# HARD TIMES

## THE WRATH OF AN ANGRY GOD

### A NOVEL BY JACK RANDOM

CROW DOG PRESS
TURLOCK CA USA

# Hard Times:

## The Wrath of an Angry God

## A Novel by Jack Random

Published by
Crow Dog Press
1241 Windsor Court
Turlock CA 95380

Cover photos by Sergey Ponomarev, New York Times, and Olafur Eliasson, Olafur Eliasson Studio.

ISBN-13: 978-0692659717
ISBN-10: 0692659714

# HARD TIMES

## THE WRATH OF AN ANGRY GOD

I can point to one or two things I have definitely learned by being hard up. I shall never again think that all tramps are drunken scoundrels, nor expect a beggar to be grateful when I give him a penny, nor be surprised if men out of work lack energy.

George Orwell
*Down and Out in Paris and London*

# A DAM WITH A THOUSAND CRACKS

At first and for a time people help. As long as they perceive themselves as outside the victim class, observers at a roadside accident, eyes above the fray, they toss bones to the needy and feel better. Not the elite of course. Not those who have the most to lose. Safe inside their gated and guarded fiefdoms, their contribution as far as they are concerned is hiring watchmen at substandard wages or paying a Mexican for lawn care and gardening and maintenance chores around the house.

When hard times come everything changes. Not all at once but gradually. One step at a time. Those who consider themselves above the storm are swept in. The victim class grows like a nasty virus that will not let go. The elite behind their guarded walls pay more for bondable labor until they can no longer spare the extra cash. Guard stations go empty, walls crumble and the elite are exposed to the multitudes.

Welcome to hard times. Hard times for everyone. No one gets a pass. The wealthy become survivors and survivors become homeless and the homeless become vagabonds and vagabonds become desperados and rise up or die. The power of the state breaks down. Like a dam with a thousand cracks it crumbles at first break.

Not with a bang but a whimper the end days come.

These are not the end days. No Cormac McCarthy post-apocalyptic hell bent story here. No one blows up the world. We just let it unfold in slow motion. We all watch from the sidelines and don't raise a hand. We don't know how. Like someone put something in the air or the water that paralyzes us from the neck down.

These are the hard times before the break when hope still resides in the heart of humankind. Scared and desperate but still beating.

When did it begin? I sit and think and scratch my brain until every cell of my cerebrum aches. I reconstruct events and run through them like an old movie on an endless loop. Still I cannot force them into a pattern that makes sense. Random events colliding like particles of light and darkness, matter and antimatter, tossing the universe into chaos. Is there anything I could have done? No doubt. But would it have made a difference? Is there anything we could have done as a people, as a nation, as a society or a global community? Of course. But we live in a bubble as if we can ignore the laws of economy, the laws of nature and the laws of order. Whenever I think about it and I often do, it enrages me and I have to put it aside.

I had a family. Have. I still do. When does a family cease to exist? Divorce? Abandonment? Till death do we part? Back then I had a family and we lived the American dream. We played by the rules. Eyes to the pavement, one step following the next. Forward. Always forward.

I worked my way from the bottom up in the construction industry. That's right, construction. Growing up my teachers and counselors told me I had the mind of a scientist with the soul of an artist. So naturally I ended up in construction. In time I started my own business as a contractor. For the first time in my life I made some real money. Not a lot but enough to feel good about it, enough to meet our needs and a little more. My wife Madge sold real estate until we had our first child, a curious little boy we named Denim. Beautiful child. I saw trouble in his bright blue eyes the first time I looked at him. Just like his father. Two years later we had our second child, a sweet little girl, Cheryl Lyn. We call her Charlie. We traded up like everyone else. Bought a bigger house and took out a loan on the value of our home.

How were we supposed to know it was a bad move? Everyone does it and everyone makes money. Remember? Stocks come and go, gold rises and falls, but real estate never fails. Never. Not in the long run. It's a game without losers. Remember? Everybody plays. Everybody wins. As sure as the sun rises in the east and dives in the west, the value of land and apartment buildings and shopping centers and suburban neighborhoods goes up and up and up.

We suffered some kind of mass delusion. How else can you explain it? Smart people doing stupid things, certain that if we all continue to pretend we can create our own reality. The banks create money out of thin air and everyone lines up to get their share. Stupidity. Stupidity combined with greed.

When you take a moment to think, we brought it on our selves. Maybe we wanted to crash the system. Or maybe we just didn't care. Kick the can down the road and let it explode on someone else's yard.

My business went bad soon after the crackdown on migrant labor. Yet another blow for the all-powerful forces of stupidity. I hired locally but I couldn't turn a profit. Madge took a part-time job selling fragrances at the mall. Not enough. Not nearly enough. We tapped out our credit cards and took out a second mortgage, then a third, but we still couldn't keep up with our debt and the ever-rising interest rates that the banks in their infinite wisdom imposed. With all their analysts and logarithms and predictive software they couldn't see the forest for the trees. They killed the golden goose and had a good laugh doing it.

The housing crash hit like a hammer to the forehead. We couldn't even afford to sell out. Like millions of others we were caught in a trap. No exit. No way forward and no way back. I lost my business and we lost our home.

Like so many others, we turned to family for refuge. We moved in with Madge's mother Grace who lived alone in a modest house, a house meant for a retired couple. She'd lost her husband in the last year.

We knew it would be tight but we thought it would only last six months, a year at the most, until we pulled ourselves together and dug out of the hole. We sold most of our belongings for what little we could get to help with the expenses and set up a living space in a spare bedroom – more like an office space or a reading room, which is exactly how Grace used it before we moved in.

I looked for another job, always two steps behind the curve. At first I looked in the construction industry but the industry was locked up. No loans, no contracts, no jobs, no openings. I looked into retraining programs and government jobs. They put me on a list. By the time I got around to service jobs, counter jockeys and floor sales, nobody had anything. It comes down to basic math: When nobody's buying you don't need anyone to sell.

Hundreds of us, thousands, all hard-working, fully functional human beings, looking for work and finding absolutely nothing. Locked out. The world of opportunity we had grown accustomed to and took for granted vanished in the tick of a clock. A time bomb waiting to explode.

I feel as bad as a man can feel. I grew up on the simple notion that if you work hard and play by the rules you can make it. You might not get rich (that idea pretty much died a long time ago) but you'd have a roof over your head, clean water, a warm bed and no one would go hungry.

As the man of the family I bear the responsibility. When it all breaks down and I can no longer take care of my family, the blame belongs to me. I own it. Of course I do. You can blame the politicians or the international corporations or greedy bankers or anyone you want (and believe me, I did and do) but it comes down to a man's responsibility, a father's duty and a husband's job. Others can waste their time with the blame game. Not me. I'm better than that. My parents raised me to be better than that.

Yeah right. Just another lie to put on the list of lies my father told me. Not his fault either. Nobody's fault. Just the way it was until it wasn't.

Angry? Yes. I'm angry. But anger only takes you

so far before it turns into something else and something else tears at your gut until it sickens you. Get on with it. Turn the page and figure out what the hell you can do about it. We adapt. That's what people do. That's about the only thing we're good at.

It seems we have a shot. We make the adjustments. We learn to live with less but we get by. Then Madge's brother Carlin shows up with his wife Joan and their three kids. Of course they move in. They have no options. What did we think was going to happen? Same thing happened to them as happened to us, only it unfolded a little slower. Happened to everyone except the old folks who held on to their homes because they were too old to refinance and couldn't be bothered. Every family in America is looking at the same story. We're damn lucky Grace didn't take that reverse mortgage deal pimped on TV by some senator who wanted to be president. If she had we'd all be out on the street.

Weeks go by and the vice gets tighter and tighter. We live on an old woman's retirement checks and wait for food stamps or some other kind of assistance that never comes. We close up the back porch with found materials we pull from scrap heaps around town, two-by-fours and plywood with rags and newspapers for insulation. Things get a little better and I start thinking we can make it.

I should have known. In this new world every time you catch a break the hammer comes down again. Sooner or later you're bound to learn: Keep your head down. Don't look ahead. Most of all, don't hope. It only breaks your spirit when the next blow hits.

Sometimes it comes like a demon in the night; other times it wears a smile and a friendly face.

Aunt Mildred and Uncle Bud show up with their hands open and their pockets empty. Of course they do. Same old story. Where else can they go? Before then we hardly ever saw them even at holidays but here they stand pleading with raw desperation for food and shelter from the storm. When times were good they sold their home and bought a Winnebago to spend the rest of their days traveling the world. When hard times came the company old Bud had given the best of his working life to, folded like a pair of deuces in Texas hold-em. He lost his pension, sold the Winnebago and ended up no better off than a common beggar.

I sit on a corner of the sofa in Grace's cramped living room and watch her try to turn them away. Knowing full well we have no more room and too many mouths to feed she looks at them and it breaks her heart. This sad elderly couple has nowhere else to go.

"We'll make do," says Grace.

And we all surrender to tears.

It comes down to numbers. After a while (I can't even remember how many weeks or months it took), I realize I have no real function. I have skills with tools but so does Carlin. He can do pretty much anything I can. The fact is I'm no longer needed. I find myself eating less and worrying more. One more bad break will push us, push me, over the edge. A time bomb.

Tick, tick, tick.

Now I'm not the kind of man who turns to crime in desperate times (though I would learn soon enough it is less a moral imperative than a cultural choice) so I don't have a lot of options. Late at night I find a quiet corner out back and write a letter to Madge and the kids. It's the hardest thing I've ever had to do.

*Dear Madge, Denim and Charlie:*

*These are hard times and we are all going to have to make sacrifices. I never would have thought that giving up and moving out could be an act of kindness but here we are. We don't have enough room and I take more than my share. We don't have enough food and I need too much just to keep going.*

*The time has come for me to make a hard choice and I've finally made it. The best thing I can do for my family and loved ones right now is to go away. Carlin can do anything I can around the house and I know I can count on Denim and Charlie to help out. You'll have a little more space and one less mouth to feed.*

*I don't know how long it will take or what I'll have to do to survive out there but I'll come back when it's all over and times are better. When that time comes I hope you'll understand what I did and why.*

*Your loving husband and father,*
*Stone.*

That's my story. History. Like most stories, long or short, the ending is only the beginning. I tell myself it has to get better. I have to believe that. No matter how dark it gets, no matter how long it takes and how many hardships we have to endure, in the end it gets better. The only thing I have to do is stay alive until the skies clear, the storm passes and I find my way home. Somewhere in the swallows of my mind a quote from

# HARD TIMES

the bible crawls into my thoughts:  God doesn't give us
any problems we can't handle.
   God, I hope that's true.

The worst sin towards our fellow creatures is not to hate them but to be indifferent to them: That's the essence of humanity.

George Bernard Shaw
*The Devil's Disciple*

# THE BRIDGE CAMP

Carrying a shoulder bag with some tools wrapped in a blanket and a small canteen, I leave the house before sunlight and walk due west, knowing that Madge will look for me in town.

Where do you go when you've got nowhere to go and nowhere to be?

You wander the streets in a fog of reflection, heart filled with remorse, brain stunted with confusion, until something happens to shock you awake. I walk through familiar streets or what used to be familiar streets, feeling more than seeing heads turn, dogs yapping and eyes sizing me up to measure whether I possess anything of greater value than the cost I would extract defending myself. I can't process the things I see, the information I gather through my senses. A stranger in a strange land, a man without bearing, borderline insane and possibly dangerous.

When my shadow disappears on the pavement I find myself on a country road lined with peach trees, almond orchards and fields of grapes on both sides. The air seems almost too thick to breathe. The smell of fallen fruit, dirt mixing with sweat on my skin, insects and microbes eager for fresh blood. The drought has not yet robbed the fields of their vitality. That will come. Down the road it will come.

I hear the rumbling low growl of a large dog, then another and a third and it stops me where I stand. I raise my gaze to see a bearded man with an aluminum baseball bat walk toward me, a hunting knife strapped to his belt. I hear the dogs attack and I think: a rabbit, a gopher, a small animal cornered in the fields. I hear the yell of a man in fear and pain and I think again. I start to go toward the sound, to help him, but the bearded man in overalls and a John Deere cap shakes his head and grips his bat, stopping maybe six feet in front of me.

"You lost, mister?"

I realize I haven't spoken in hours, haven't eaten or had a drink of water. I haven't sat for a moment's rest. I can't find my voice. I shake my head and clear my throat.

"I'm walking."

"I can see that."

I watch him take stock of me. He doesn't believe I pose a threat. Still he gives my bag a second look. I can see he takes no joy in what he's doing but he has a job in a world that has none to offer. Simple as that.

"You look like a harmless fellow. I'm going to give you some good advice. You can take it or not. That's up to you."

He turns and looks west down the road, one of those endless roads that vanishes like a mirage in the distant hills.

"You can keep walking down this road. Eventually you're going to get hungry and wander off to grab a peach, maybe some grapes, whatever. When you do those dogs will hunt you down. I don't need to tell you what happens then."

The dogs come trotting up, licking their chops, behind their owner. Something taints the air like a foul breath and I can only guess it's fear or blood. Some poor man's groans out in the fields subside to the point you can no longer hear him. Silence. Sickening, pleading silence.

"That man needs help."

"Don't you worry about no man but your self. You keep walking down this road, nothing good can come of it."

He watches me think and knows I'm convinced.

"You from around here?"

"Yes."

"You know the Seventh Street Bridge?"

I nod. When we were kids, we used to run around down there.

"There's a camp there. Lots of folks just like you. Got nowhere else to go."

I nod.

"You go there. At the very least, you'll have a place to sleep tonight."

So that's how I came to be living under a bridge with dozens of other lost souls, upwards of ninety all toll. Another hundred or so across the river.

I've been here two or three months now and it's changed me. It's changed the way I look at things and what I think. I've become a part of the community. I've learned that misfortune has nothing to do with character. We work hard every day and we take care of each other. We all have a story. Every one of us.

I write them down in little notebooks and on scraps of paper I find in garbage dumps and alleys. I don't know why but I feel it's important. It makes me feel more human somehow. It makes me feel like people matter even though the whole damned world says we don't.

Bridges used to be mostly for transportation. Now it seems like they serve mostly as shelters. A man tells me that if you wait here long enough and manage to stay alive (good luck with that), you'll meet everyone you ever knew right here under the bridge. I thought it was funny in a wry sort of way but after a few more weeks, I came to believe it.

How do we survive? This river still has some catfish, mud daubers and other edible fish. Everything we catch goes in the pot. Some of the wild orchards around here still give fruit and nuts. The river's running low these days but we've got plenty of water to keep things growing. We have a greenhouse for growing vegetables. Everything goes in the pot. If you don't share you get booted out. That's how I got my spot. Some poor soul got caught hording and the camp booted him out just when I showed up. I thank God they didn't keep a waiting list.

Every month or so a truck shows up with guards, handing out blankets, jackets, flour and dried fruit. That's what remains of government service. The people of the bridge know they work for the government because their guards carry guns.

One of the last effective acts of government was to confiscate all the ammunition. Ironic, isn't it? The second amendment to the constitution protects the right to own guns but it says nothing about ammunition. You can have all the firearms you want. You can collect them, horde them, keep them shiny and clean, put one under your pillow and two on the wall but you can't have the bullets to fill them up.

Naturally, the militias and gun owners didn't go down without a fight. When the media was still up every station of every conduit from CNN to the Daily Web Cam filled every hour of every day with raging battles between private citizens and their government. At first they called on the police, then the National Guard, then the army and Special Forces. Plenty of soldiers switched sides. It's never easy to pull the trigger on your own people. No one knows how many died in those battles but in the end they pretty much disarmed the entire citizenry.

The government offered food for bullets and gas for guns and when the supply of both diminished the militias and the NRA activists and the gun-toting cowboys gave way. People have to eat and find shelter. The hardcore survivalists headed for the hills and holed up as long as they could but in most places game had already been hunted out. The age of ideology is dead and gone. Replaced by a survival ethic. Every man, every woman and every family has to take care of their own.

Those of us who end up under the bridge learn to make do with what we have. Everyone gets their fair share. We have a guest space that people can use for a few days. After that, unless a spot opens up, you have to move on. No one remembers who came up with the rules but we all live by them.

There have been a number of attempts to take the bridge over – thugs, gangsters and other types who are used to getting their way. Each time the people here came together to defend the camp.

We have quite a collection of weapons: clubs, spears, knives, axes, hatchets, tools, chains, pipes and crowbars, anything you can think of to fight with short of firearms and explosives.

People have camps all over town, in every park, in abandoned buildings and parking lots. The last I heard people stay away from the malls but who knows. As a rule they're a poor place to find what you need to sustain life. No food, no water and all the merchandise, clothes, blankets, generators, batteries, tools and electronics have long been cleaned out. Businesses carted everything off in trucks to store them in remote warehouses with guard dogs and razor wire and wait for the day when things have real monetary value again. It'll be a long wait.

Do I think about my family? Yes. At first, every minute of every day. But after a while you learn to push it back. If you get caught daydreaming around here you pay a price. Some say you have to live in the moment. That may work for them but I've learned my own way. You have to *be* in the moment but you have to *think* ahead – not too far of course but just ahead, like headlights on a dark road. Once you've taken care of your needs for the day, you take care of tomorrow and the next day – if you can manage it.

Just the same, in the late evenings when all the work that can be done has been done, I make a point of getting to know the people I live, work, eat and sleep with. I find that people generally like to talk and if you're willing to listen they tell you their stories. I take them in and remember them until I find time to write them down. People think I'm a bit touched for wasting my time and maybe I am but that's the job I've chosen and I'll stick to it.

Most people who come to the camp come alone. That's just a fact. Couples break up under the strain.

But one couple I met managed to stay together through it all. They arrived at the camp that way. I think that makes them a real love story.

Their names are Willie and Marguerite. They lost their apartment and went to a shelter. When the shelter got too crowded, as they all did, the caretaker asked Willie to leave. Willie did nothing wrong but hard choices had to be made. They decided to keep the women and children. Marguerite could have stayed but she went with him.

"We been together thick and thin, sickness and health. Aint nobody going to tear us under." That's how Marguerite put it.

They ended up out on the streets, begging and living day to day, until they found their way to the bridge where eventually they made their stand. You never see Willie without Marguerite. They go fishing together. They work in the garden together. They eat together and sleep together. Willie almost killed a man who tried to come between them and no one around here would have blamed him. Justice among the lost and forgotten. The way it is.

Marguerite migrated from Mexico as a child – legal or illegal, nobody cares any more. Willie grew up in this valley and found work as a trucker. Marguerite took a job as a waitress at a roadside café where Willie stopped for coffee and a piece of pie. Thinking she didn't speak English, Willie told her she was the most beautiful woman he'd ever laid eyes on after the Grand Canyon. A smile led to an invitation. She hung up her apron and jumped in his cab. Thirty-six years later they've never been apart.

Willie and Marguerite, Stone and Madge: two different stories and both without ends. It almost makes you want to cry.

If I were a praying man, I'd pray that Willie and Marguerite die on the same breath, wrapped in each other's arms, in a warm place many years into the future when the harshness of these days is only a memory. At the same time, I'd pray that someday I'll find my way back to Madge and the kids in better times. I'll ask their forgiveness and, God willing, we'll live a long and fruitful life.

I spend a lot of time worrying about Madge and the kids. I try to talk myself into going back but I always work my way around to the same conclusion. Without some way to help out I would only end up back on the street looking for a place a whole lot worse than the one I've got. Maybe someday things will change. That's what everyone here hopes and prays.

I met a man named Riggs here. I'm guessing that's his last name but I don't know for sure. I'm pleased to call him my friend. He has his kid Ronan with him. This camp is not any kind of a place for a kid but Ronan, like his father, is tough as nails. Works as hard as anyone twice his age and never complains. When I ask how they ended up here, they both shrug, Ronan after his dad, and Riggs says: *Just lucky I guess.*

I learn from someone who knew him before the crash that Riggs was a single father for as long as anyone knew. Rumor has it his wife either overdosed or went back to her old lifestyle, doing what she has to do for the drugs she needs. Riggs still pines for her but he never says a word. Whenever the subject of wives or relationships comes up, sadness sweeps over him like a dark shadow and he withdraws from the world until it passes.

24

# HARD TIMES

He worked as a foreman at the canning plant before it shut down. He had no family in the area and he didn't believe in government assistance so when they lost the house, he and Ronan took to the streets together. The kid is a free spirit who likes to run and, as much as Riggs admires him for it, he never lets him out of his sight. If Ronan ducks behind a corner or disappears behind some bushes hunting berries, Riggs stops whatever he's doing and moves to where he can see his kid. No one doubts he would kill or be killed to protect his son and that alone is protection enough in the Bridge Camp.

Ronan loves sports and games so someone usually organizes a game of soccer or stickball after the workday before the sun goes down. As the only kid in camp, we all look after him. We help him, teach him when we can, and take pride in the way he carries himself. In many ways he belongs to all of us.

The fact is we all look after each other. We've become a kind of family. Of course most of us had a family before hard times and we all hope this new life doesn't last long. It ties us together: More than anything else we want to go home. We want to go back to a way of life that no longer exists.

Everyone has a story. Everyone had a life before this life. But it's always a story about the past or the present. No one speaks of the future. There are not many hopes and dreams in this camp except the hope that we live through the night. We seem incapable of looking forward. We can see what lies immediately in front of us, as far as we can without losing hold of the present, and we look no further. We take steps to ensure our safety, our warmth, our food supply and whatever else we need. But we don't talk about our plans. We're here now and that's as far as it goes.

I'm thinking maybe I should hit the road. Every few days I see family members come down to the camp looking for their lost fathers. It's almost always the fathers they come looking for. I listen to them talk. I watch them try to hide their emotions. Children are the worst. They cannot begin to understand. They don't know what it means for a parent to be a burden.

It usually works. The father goes back to the family and does whatever he can to be useful. He learns to cook and clean and tries not to eat any more than he needs to stay alive. After a few weeks he's usually back out on the streets. No emotions or sense of duty can change the cold hard reality we have to live with and accept for the good of all involved.

I don't want that to happen to me. I think about it every night, all night, and most of the day. I know the day will come when Madge comes to understand but the kids are still too young. It's only a matter of time before Charlie shows up, pleading with her wide beautiful eyes, crying when I resist, arguing when I try to explain. I know I would have to give in but I also know how it will turn out. The hammer of destiny awaits me.

If I saw my children going hungry because of me, I know what it would do to me. I'd rather be a bum than a thief. And I'd rather be out under a bridge than in some jail. It's not so easy to get thrown in jail these days anyway. The cops would rather shoot you than give you free food and shelter. They take you out of town and tell you to keep moving. If they catch you again they give you a beating and take you ten, twenty miles out. The jails are past full. No one gets in unless someone gets out. So much for the zero tolerance three-strikes laws. If it was easy to get locked up, half the population would be there. Maybe more.

I'm thinking of traveling east, going to Denver to see my parents, to see how things are going there. I tell myself it might be different. Maybe the government is still functioning there. Maybe food and clean water are more plentiful. Maybe I can help. The last I heard everyone was fine – or at least they said they were.

I realize I should have called while the lines were still working but I was afraid it would cut off my options. As long as I can believe it might be better, it keeps my spirits up. A traveler needs the strength of hope – especially if he has no money.

Word is the roads are jammed with hitchhikers. It's a basic law of human nature: irrational optimism. It has to be better down the road. Or maybe we're beyond that. Even if it isn't better and no matter how bad it gets, it's still better to keep moving. As long as we're moving, we're still alive and that's all the hope we can get.

I've talked to people who've been out there. They all say the same thing: Don't go. It's better here than it is out there. It's dangerous and decent shelter is hard to find. But if I have my mind set, they tell me to stay off the main highways as much as possible and don't take just any ride. It's sound advice when times are good. It's critical when times are hard and you never know who you can trust or who might cut your throat for a pair of shoes.

So I think about it, wrestle with it, turn it around in every sector of my mind and examine it from every angle, determined not to let it walk away without a good fight. When the time comes, if it comes at all, I will be ready. I'll do everything I can to prepare. In the meantime, I'll make myself useful by gathering stories of good, hard working people that society discarded under a bridge.

# SUGAR FROM INDIANA

When I think of all the bad things that happen to good people, it breaks my heart. I guess a part of me feels a little better about my own situation when I realize that people far better than me have suffered far greater misfortune.

I meet a lot of people in the Bridge Camp that I'll never forget but the best of them is a man named Sugar, born and raised in the great state of Indiana, in a little town outside of Gary. He's a fix it man. He worked on the farms, in the towns and cities, repairing everything from tractors to assembly lines. You name it he can fix it. He married his high school sweet heart, had a kid and saved enough money to start his own business. He worked as hard as any man does and eventually bought a home. He thought he was doing just fine until his son grew up, got married and took off for California and the dream of a better life. Sugar reflects with a shake of his head and eyes full of sorrow that California is about as far as you could get from Indiana without leaving the country.

His wife left him. After all those many years, too many to count without falling into despair, she said she never really knew him and never had a chance to fall in love. Looking back, he has to admit he spent too much time working and not enough attending to family. It amazes me how often these things happen to good, kind-hearted people. It's as if there's some kind of quota on how much good you can do or how much care you can give to others. If you give too much to strangers, you fall behind at home. If you give too much at home, you fall short in the world. Like everything else, it's about balance.

That's just one of the things Sugar learned when it was too late to do anything about it. He went into a tailspin. He lost his business but managed to hold on to his home by doing what he'd always done. He fixed things by day and drank by night. By the time hard times hit the rest of the country he was already a lost cause. For him it was a wake up call. He lost his house but he sobered up and discovered a deep-seated need to reconnect with his son. So he hit the road and made his way over the highways and byways of a crumbling nation, eventually finding his way to the great central valley of California.

He never did find his son. He found a place where he used to live but he and his wife were long gone. Scattered like dry leaves on an autumn wind. Well, at least he tried. He takes some solace in that. It's a miserable consolation but it's all he has left. That's how he ended up under a bridge with a whole lot of people just like him. People who worked hard their whole lives but ended up drawing the short end of the stick. Just the way it goes.

It's hard times for everyone but people like Sugar take hold of it with both hands. For him it's another start and another chance to get it right. He breathes it in, embraces it, and sets about trying to make life better for everyone around him.

I felt a strong connection with Sugar the first time we met. Most people lose the big picture when they hit the streets. They become self-centered, oriented to survival and nothing else. Sugar is different. I saw it him right away. He cares about people. He cares about animals too and treats both with respect.

Sugar is a dog man and there are about six or seven dogs and a good dozen cats in camp at any given time. They all have names, they're all smart enough to survive on their own and Sugar knows every one of them. He spends about as much time with dogs as with people. As a general rule he prefers the company of dogs to humans and women to men and he doesn't trust any man who doesn't feel the same way.

When I ended up under the bridge with the rest of the vagabonds, Sugar kept his distance and watched me for a while. He saw that I went by the rules and wasn't afraid of work. He saw that I had a habit of collecting stories, always writing things down on scraps of paper, tucking them away in my coat pocket or in the travel bag I carry. He finds it interesting that I spend my precious time on a lost art, writing what no one will ever read. He saw that I was a good listener and that was a quality he could appreciate. Sugar's a good talker.

He likes to talk about his adventures and one night we found ourselves sitting side by side in a fire circle and he told me his story. Now we talk every night. I talk about my plans and all the things that worry me. It seems I'm always worried about something. He relates his experiences on the road, points of danger and exhilaration, lessons learned and lessons lost. Mostly he tries to teach me the things I need to know if I want to survive out there on my own. He teaches me slow and easy, by metaphor and allegory, not like a preacher handing down the word from on high but more like an older brother who's been around the block.

I asked him one time if Sugar was his real name. He smiled and said it wasn't. It's the name his wife gave him. He prefers it to his given name so he kept it. He never told me what his real name is.

When I tell him about my plan to leave camp with the idea of making it to Colorado to see my parents, I know Sugar thinks it's a lame idea but he never says so out loud. A man should have a goal in mind, some sense of destiny, even if his idea of destiny never pulls him that far. There are a lot of people on the road these days, more than there ever have been. Most of them are good people caught up in hard times but even a good man can do bad things if he's desperate enough and there is a lot of desperation going around. Some individuals are just born to do bad things and there are plenty of those as well.

"You develop a sixth sense and you learn to trust it," he says in his deep chiseled voice. "Listen to it. If it tells you something's wrong, something's wrong. Lots of people out there are looking to take what you got."

He says there are people in the woods everywhere you go. They set up shelters built of plywood and sheets of tin, tents and corrugated cardboard.

"Most of them will take you in for a night but don't overstay your welcome. That's what they're afraid of. That you'll hang around and become some kind of leach. The moment you see that hint of fear and worry, it's time to move on."

He tells stories of being stranded on remote desert highways, being surrounded by a pack of wild hungry dogs, hoodlums who shook him down for a roll of postage stamps and abandoned him by the roadside in the middle of nowhere.

"People are good at heart," he reflects, his mind drifting to places and times mostly forgotten. "I still believe that. But when hard times come something takes hold of them. People that never stole anything in their lives will take your last crumb of bread. It's a cold world out there, boy. You got to keep your head up and your senses alive."

Sugar tells me I was what he considered an easy mark when I came into camp but as time went by I became a little wiser and a lot more cautious. I learn by watching people coming and going, seeing how they act and knowing who to trust. Sugar helps me along and I take his advice like a religious man takes the gospel. He tells me places to go and places to avoid. He tells me what to pack and what not to bother with. The premium is weight and durability. Dried goods and sardine cans and hard candy are good. Cans of soup and fruit and vegetables are too heavy.

"Eat 'em and leave 'em," he says. A pouch for water instead of a canteen. "Got to have clean drinking water."

We spend a lot of time talking about weapons or what could be used to defend your self from desperate humans and hungry beasts. He advises me to get a good strong walking stick.

"It don't threaten people but it gives them pause if they've got a mind to roll you."

"A good knife will serve you but keep it strapped to your leg and out of sight. It's there if you need it but don't show no one your hand before it's played."

He shows me how to roll my stuff up in a couple of

good lightweight blankets, bind them with strips of leather and hang it over my shoulder.

"You'll want a good hat," he says. "One with plenty of brim that clings to your head in a strong wind. Can't say enough about a good hat."

I gather things I think I'll need, including maps I pull out of the dumps.

Then one day Sugar takes stock of all I have and how much I've learned and he gives me a wink.

"You're ready. As ready as you'll ever be."

It's late summer and Sugar senses that I'm about to make my move. He figures whatever happens the most likely scenario is we'll never see each other again. I'm just another story to be told, a speculation and a mystery. In the days and months ahead Sugar will stop at peculiar times, tending the garden or building a fence, and wonder where I am and whether or not I actually made a run at the Great Rocky Mountains. A tough go if there ever is one. There will be times he'll wonder if I'm still alive and he'll say a little prayer hoping that I am. I'll wonder the same about him. There's a connection between us and that will remain as long as either of us walks the earth.

We shake hands and I set out walking due east the next morning at the crack of dawn. A teenage kid is staking my spot the moment I check out. I tip my hat and wish him well. There's a lot fear in the kid's eyes and I know he's afraid I'll change my mind.

I almost do. It isn't easy leaving behind a place of safety, a place where people pull together and actually help each other, and a place where I'd formed lasting friendships. It occurs to me it might be the dumbest thing I've ever done. But once I walk out, there's no turning back.

It is fatal to look hungry. It makes people want to kick you.

George Orwell
*Down and Out in Paris and London*

# THE ROAD

I get out of town and walk all day on country roads heading more or less east, staying away from the big orchards and vineyards, stopping only when I see an opportunity for food. I find some berries along a creek bed and some peaches just short of ground rot in an old untended orchard. I sit down to eat and rest my weary bones. By the look of the sun there's no more than an hour or so of sunlight left. I figure I've walked a good ten to twelve hours at a decent pace, covering thirty miles or more. My legs ache, my feet are sore and my mind is clouded with second thoughts so I decide to call it a day.

All day long I've seen only four vehicles: three of them heading the other way, the other an old Ford pickup. I don't know if it's the price of gas or the fact that gas at any price is too much but the problem of traffic congestion has disappeared. Most gas stations have gone out of business and those that remain are only open a few days a week.

Hard times change the way you look at yourself and the way you look at others. You see things you never would have noticed before. You make judgments based on little things, a tilt of the head, a gleam in the eyes or the way a man turns to hide what he's thinking.

The driver of the Ford, a man maybe a little older than me with a green John Deere cap, slowed down to look me over. It seems to me the man was worried that I was walking in the direction of his home, his garden or the orchard he took care of and wanted to be sure I wasn't a thief. I tipped my hat but I did not stick my thumb out. I didn't trust him and I wasn't ready for a ride. I want time to think without having to deal with other people. In the back of my mind maybe I don't want to go too far in case I have a change of heart.

I gather some wood and kindling for a fire and lay out my blankets a ways off the road. I have an old copy of George Stewart's *Earth Abides* that I traded *The Grapes of Wrath* for on the grounds that it weighs less but I don't feel like reading so I just sit here gazing at the sun as it sinks below the cottonwoods in the western sky.

I light a fire as the sun goes down, more for light than warmth, and after a while I get a feeling I'm being watched. I pull out my knife and start whittling and keep my walking stick at hand just in case. A while later I hear a whimpering and realize there's a dog sitting in the dark, keeping its distance, scouting me out, looking for someone to partner with.

Dogs and cats, pets of all kinds, had it bad when hard times hit. Most of the vicious dogs that lost their owners, the pit bulls and Rottweilers that served as guard dogs, were euthanized or shot down before the ammunition ban. The pounds and shelters are full and charging fees so people discard them in the country. It made me mad until I thought it through. What else can they do? If times get any worse God forbid people will start eating their animals and the animals will turn on them. Dog eat dog is not just a saying.

I get on my haunches and make a clicking sound, holding my hand out to call her to me. She moves slowly out of the shadows into the light of the fire and I can see she's a small to medium dog, golden with white patches and floppy ears, maybe a border collie mix. She's not a pup but she's young and scared. She backs off twice before she comes to me, licks my hand and looks me straight in the eyes. We connect and both of us know we have a partner like it or not.

Growing up the family had a couple of dogs and I had a dog as a younger man, all of them mutts. I like dogs. I admire them. That kind of loyalty might be bred but it's an amazing thing to behold. A dog will go up against a mountain lion to protect its people. A dog will walk a thousand miles to get back home. A dog will stay with you when you're sick and run with you in bad weather. There are all kinds of dogs and all kinds of humans but the best dogs are those that choose you like this dog chooses me.

Now I have a new line of problems to think about: dog problems. Giving her a good name, making sure she gets enough to eat and keeping her out of danger. I think about a leash but that seems ridiculous under the circumstances. I'm not her master, her owner or even her protector. She's a free agent just like me. Any time she wants to move on that's her business. I have no say in it.

It occurs to me as she lays with her head on my lap while I scratch behind her ears that she'll keep me warm when the weather turns cold. I have no idea how a dog like her would fare in the wild. Probably not much better than a city man like me. But maybe I'm getting the better end of the deal. She's a good dog, a smart dog, and as long as she stays with me I will not be alone.

I try to remember the dog's name in the old Harlan Ellison story *A Boy and His Dog* without success. In the days before the crash you could look up information like that on the web. Not now. The web is down and out. There's no one to man the stations for an enterprise that produces nothing of tangible value. So the age of information is pretty much over – at least for the masses. A modern day dark ages has begun. Maybe it's for the best. A dog should find its own name or at least it shouldn't be saddled with something from our sordid past.

I sleep with one eye open most of the night. When I wake up the dog is gone. I figure she must have had her own second thoughts and moved on. But then she comes running with her tail up, bright eyes, smiling like a dog smiles. She has something in her mouth and places it in my hand. It's a blueberry. That's a good dog. She's learned to scavenge and saves one for her new partner. I thank her and pull out a piece of jerky I'd stowed away. We split it down the middle.

Things are looking up.

My plan is to turn south and I figure the turnoff is no more than a few miles down the road. There are no easy ways to cross the Sierras or the Rockies so I decide to cross the desert at Death Valley, follow Route 66 to New Mexico and turn north to Colorado.

That's the plan but in the back of my mind I understand that everything is malleable. Now more than ever. I resolve to remain open to whatever experiences unfold. My official destination is Denver but I have no expectations. In all likelihood I will stay a few days or a week and go my way. I have no intention of imposing on my blood family any more than I have on my married family. Times are hard everywhere and the least I can do is not add to the burden. If I can help I'll do what I can. If not, I'm back on the road.

I have a dog now and she's full of spirit. She takes my mind from my worries. After a while I decide to name her Cinnamon after an old Neil Young song. The song always gives me a lift. Walking down the road trying to keep my mind open and my senses clear my Cinnamon Girl jogs before me like she's royalty. She's full of joy and hyped with energy. It must have broken someone's heart to let her go.

After an hour or so we turn south according to plan and keep walking. Another hour and a truck comes up behind us and slows. It's the same man who passed me yesterday.

"You want a ride?"

"I've got a dog."

"I noticed."

I look him over and decide he's probably okay. We both jump in the cab, Cinnamon in the middle. His name is Frank. He's a little fidgety and strange as if unaccustomed to casual conversation – at least with strangers. He explains that he's delivering food packages to town and apologizes for not picking me up before. I shrug and say I'd probably have done the same. I hope it it's not true but it probably is. Hard times teach you to be cautious. Everyone wants something. Everyone has an angle. Everyone except a man and his dog.

He tells me he has a farm in the country. It's a kind of cooperative with about two dozen people. They grow apples, pears, peaches, almonds and assorted garden vegetables. They're self sufficient he relates with a measure of pride.

He asks where I'm from and I tell him. He inquires about my story and I give him an abbreviated version. The man keeps looking in the rearview mirror and glancing sideways to catch my eyes. There's a vague sense of being interviewed and I'm not sure I like it. He starts rambling on about the good they're doing, living in harmony off the land, working together in a common enterprise, how food and labor are the only things that matter now.

I ask if it's a commune and the man laughs. It's his land, his farm and his equipment and the people who work it are working for him. I ask how much he pays and the man looks at me like I'm out of my mind. They work for food and shelter. No one has money he says. It's all about surviving in hard times.

Maybe so but I don't think he's delivering food to town for free. He volunteers that they only get what they need to keep things running: fuel to keep the generators going, clothes, blankets, light bulbs and stuff they can't grow.

We drive on for about forty-five minutes when he pulls over to the side of road.

"This is where I turn off. The farm's about ten more miles down there," he explains, pointing to the west.

If it is a job interview I figure I've done all I can to scuttle my prospects but here he is giving it one more shot.

"You're welcome to join us," he offers with a weak smile. Cinnamon is crawling over me to get out the door.

"I appreciate that," I lie. "We'll take our chances on the road."

I consider that I might be wrong but I have a bad feeling about this whole venture. These are hard times, sure, but I'm not ready for some modern day version of slavery. What else can you call working for food and shelter? Of course, it isn't slavery if you're free to leave any time you want but I'm not willing to take that chance ten miles down the road and neither is Cinnamon.

The man pulls out a couple of bags of dried pears and another of trail mix from under his seat and hands them to me like a peace offering. I thank him most sincerely and the man drives off with a nod of his head.

"Good luck, you'll need it."

I watch him drive down a one-way road kicking up dust and I have to wonder if I might come to regret my decision. A steady supply of food and a roof over your head is a powerful temptation. Cinnamon yelps and starts down the road south. I can tell she's thinking what I'm thinking: something wrong about that man.

I start walking but my mind stays behind on that truck to the farm and the fidgety man who wants to recruit me. Why? Surely there is no shortage of desperate people willing to work for food and shelter. In fact, there are too many. If he shows up at one of the camps in town looking for volunteers it might start a riot and everyone would know about it. Someone would follow the trail and the location of a critical source of food would be known. If times really got tough, townspeople would converge on the farm and take what they need. He has to pick up strays – individuals like me who for whatever reason wander away from the crowds.

I feel a desire to turn around, go back and walk down that road just to see for myself what's going on. I weigh the options. If I go back it'll consume at least two days probably three and the winter will be that much closer. After that there would be no traveling. It's hunker down, stay warm and survive. Then again, I have no real expectations of the journey to Colorado. In all likelihood I would find the same situation there as I have at home. I would be a burden on my own family. It would be a cold winter in Colorado so it really doesn't matter if I never make it out of California. I have already accomplished my objective. I'm out of the way. My wife and children cannot find me. Even if I settle on a farm in the country it's all but impossible to track me down.

On the other hand, if I go down to the farm and find what I half expect to find, what can I do about it? The authorities such as they are have no interest. The farm provides food. If they do so on the backs of slave labor that's just an unfortunate effect of the times. Then again, my job or my purpose or my chosen role in these times is to tell the story. If I do not go down that road the story might never be told.

I'm still hesitant to turn around. There's something in my head about the code of the road, the cardinal law of every pilgrim, journeyman and wandering hobo: Don't turn back. Whatever happens, whatever goes down, keep on moving. Keep on keeping on.

My self-inflicted dilemma is resolved when I come to a dirt path, a walking path that meanders off in a westward direction. I kneel down and take Cinnamon by the ears: *I know you don't want to go down there, girl. I don't blame you. But I've got to go down there and have a look. You're free to follow or free to go.*

I know she understands. Her tail stops wagging and she stares into my eyes, trying to change my mind until she realizes it's a hopeless cause. I start walking down the path and she stands there on the road for maybe twenty seconds before she trots up behind me. I kneel down, give her a good petting and kiss her forehead. She has made her decision: She will stick with me no matter what ignorant and wrong-headed decisions I make. For that I will always be grateful.

We spend the day walking through the woods, taking time to hunt for berries and sitting down for snacks from our varied food supply. Finally we come to a clearing: a small valley below the ledge where we're hiking. It's late in the daylight hours and people are still working the gardens and orchards below. The workers look tired from the day's labor but there's nothing remarkable about their appearance. Some pick fruit or vegetables and put them in baskets or bags. At the far end of the valley there's a large two-story white wood house and to its side a row of small structures – cabins or shacks – and behind them two large structures that I surmise are a barn and a warehouse. Three workers are building a new shack for what I assume are workers quarters. Another medium-sized structure I figure they use for processing, cleaning, drying and packaging. There are workers carrying bags and baskets from the fields out back. A couple of workers run water from a well to the house. All in all, it looks like a well-planned, well-run operation.

At sunset a woman emerges from the big house and rings a bell as all the workers walk from their stations to their living quarters. A while later lights go on in the shacks and the big white house. I can see two generators, one by the house and another by the first shack. About an hour later another bell rings and all the workers go out back for what I assume is a group meal. Another hour and they go back to their quarters. Another hour and the lights are replaced by flickering candlelight everywhere but the big house. I note that the workers cabins are segregated by sex with three or four assigned to each one.

I'm determined to go down for a closer look. No one is standing guard (an indication no one knows about this place) but several people linger on the porch of the big house. A couple (probably the man from the truck and his wife) is on the balcony upstairs. Under the light of a half moon, we follow the trail all the way around the fields to the back of the house where the trail ends in a descent to the valley floor.

I take a quick look inside the warehouse where row after row of boxes are neatly stacked, waiting for delivery to needy townspeople. I resist the temptation to stock up on dry goods. Keenly aware that the time might come, I'm not ready to take that leap. I'll hold on to my sense of decency as long as I can. I look in the second building and see it's divided into two sections, one for drying and packaging, the other with a complete kitchen, tables and chairs for serving meals.

We move over to the cabins away from the big house. They're constructed of plywood walls painted in uniform gray, definitely not up to the standard of cabins. These are shacks with walls so thin we can hear the voices of the workers clear enough to understand most of what is said.

I motion to Cinnamon to be quiet as we settle behind a shack where a man is talking about the segregation rule. He's angry that two willing people are not free to share a bed and a living quarter. He's angry at being confined to a small space shared with others he did not choose and who had not chosen him.

He's angry at the authority held over him by the man who rules the farm. Another man tries to talk him down, urging him to be quiet and reminding him that life outside is hard. The man just doesn't seem to care. He wants to leave. He wants to leave first thing in the morning.

"No one leaves," the other man says. "You think you can leave. They tell you you can but you can't. They put you in the rehab box and they keep you there until you change your mind. The only ones who leave are the ones who can't carry their weight. Too old or too sick. Too stubborn or feeble. Then they tell you to leave and they take you a hundred miles so you can't tell anyone about it."

The first man thinks about what he said before he offers a final comment: "Aint a man alive can keep me here against my will."

A knock on the wall, probably a signal, the candle is snuffed and silence follows.

Almost immediately Cinnamon begins to growl. Before I can bolt I'm staring at a flashlight. I make out three men silhouetted in the darkness as I slowly stand up. A voice orders me to drop my walking stick and Cinnamon goes crazy. She dashes toward them and begins a side-to-side maneuver. She's as fast and quick as the punch you never saw coming. I kneel back down and call her. I'm a little surprised when she comes to me. She recognizes the man with the flashlight before I do. It's the man in the truck that gave us a ride.

"Well, well," the man begins. "Did you change your mind or did you come here to steal some food?"

"Why would I do that?"

I have no need for any more food than I can carry.

46

Any fool would know that but I explain it to him slow and easy. As I'm talking, a group of people comes up behind me and one of them speaks out as I calm Cinn.

"Let him go," the man says. It's the same voice we heard talking inside the workers shack, the one who wants to leave if he can't room with his woman. Two more men and a woman line up behind him. Maybe more behind them, I can't tell.

"This man is trespassing," the Boss Man says.

"Call the police," someone says and everyone behind them laughs. What police are left can't be bothered with something like this. Anything short of a riot or gunshots gets a pass unless it's in the finest of neighborhoods. Even then.

I relate my situation, tell them all how the Boss Man picked us up and asked me to work on the farm and why I turned it down. I explain why I decided to have a look for myself, because I feel a duty to tell the story and I want to know the truth.

"No harm, no foul," the man from the shack says.

"You were right about this place," a woman adds.

"Aint nothing but a slave operation."

Suddenly the Boss Man is on his heels, a little concerned with the turn of affairs and the possibility of a worker revolt staring him in the face. Who knows on which side the two big men behind him would turn?

"Alright!" the Boss Man protests. "I've told you all a dozen times or more: Every one of you is free to go! But if you go you won't be welcomed back!"

You can feel the power of his words. This is a place where they're pretty much guaranteed the two things they need most: food and shelter.

"Even slaves could couple up," a workingman says.

"You've got a point," replies the Boss Man. "We'll

talk about it in the morning."

"This man free to go?"

The Boss Man nods and starts walking back to the big house. I tip my hat to the working people and thank them for taking up my cause.

"I wish we could build a fire and offer up some warm food and drink but that would stir up more trouble than it's worth," says the man who spoke up for us.

"I understand," I reply and I do. The last thing I want to do is to create a problem for these people. We shake hands and I start walking out the way we came in with Cinnamon tagging along behind me.

"Fuck it!" the man says.

I turn around and the man waves us back. He introduces himself as Leon and his buddy as Buck. The rest of them offer their own names and they lead us to a clearing east of the worker shacks. We gather wood and light a fire not for warmth but for the kind of camaraderie a campfire builds. One by one and two by two, as the fire burns, the rest of the workers come out and join the circle.

I tell them my story and they tell me theirs. Half of us have the same story. Too many mouths to feed. Too many bodies to shelter. We had to leave for the good of the family, for the good of the house or the good of the community. The other half was forced out. No hard feelings. Just the way it is when the lifeboat is treading water.

They're the outcasts and I'm one of them.

If you're in trouble or hurt or need, go to the poor people. They're the only ones that'll help.

John Steinbeck
*The Grapes of Wrath*

# THE FARM

Leon grew up in a city on a hill where his parents bought a home. It wasn't much but it was theirs and they were proud of it. His parents came from Chicago and like their parents before them they worked for black people with money. His grandparents came from Mississippi where they worked as sharecroppers, and their parents came from Louisiana where they toiled as slaves. Over the years and across the generations the family grew three shades lighter and lost a lot of their African features but that slave blood still runs through his veins and informs him who he is.

His parents didn't live long enough to see every last thing they worked so hard for – their home, their savings and their dreams – come crashing down like a tin shack in a hurricane wind. His mother died of complications from diabetes and his father died of a heart condition. Leon reflected the condition was when his wife died he would too.

They had five kids, three boys and two girls, and Leon was the youngest. One by one they got out of Chicago to escape the wars: the drug wars, the street wars, the gang wars, the crime wars and the wars against the wars. It seems there's always a war on something or someone. If there weren't, you wouldn't need politicians. Politicians invent wars so they can pretend to be warriors.

They all migrated west to the great central valley of California where they thought things would be better but they weren't. They scattered like dandelion seeds in the wind. Someday Leon swore he'd find out what happened to his brothers and sisters or die trying. I have no doubt that day will come. Meantime, he ended up on The Farm.

Leon was born to be a leader. Women listen to him and men understand what he's talking about. It usually works out in his favor. Everywhere you go you find people who stand up when times are rough. Leon stood up for me because he sensed that I would do the same for him. He needs allies in his fight against the Boss Man and he sees that potential in me.

I'm flattered. I'd like to believe I'm the kind of man you can count on in a fight but I'm also the kind of man who likes to find another way. I've seen too many fights in my time, usually people against people who shouldn't be enemies. Leon tells me the workers saved my hide because they could tell by sixth sense I was meant to save theirs. I tell him I'm just a man trying to do the best I can in a bad situation. He just smiles like he knows something I don't, his big brown eyes shining with firelight.

Leon is a big man with big strong hands. He never had trouble finding work before hard times came. He tells anyone who will listen "hard times" doesn't do it justice.

"This here is a great depression no different than the pictures you see in the history books. That's how I came to be working in a slave operation. It has to be *real* hard times. Men like me and Buck wouldn't suffer such indignities unless we had no choice."

That's what they think and tell themselves every day of the week and twice on Sundays. They have no choice. They're wrong, as wrong as wrong can be. I believe that's why I came along. To tell them what they should already know: you always have a choice. I believe we all know it in our hearts but we push that part of our souls away from our minds and daily lives. We know there are things we would do to survive, things we would be ashamed of doing and want to hide, but one thing we can never do is give up being human. As long as we have a choice, we remain human. When we no longer have a choice, when we sacrifice that basic part of ourselves, we're no better than farm animals. Or worse, we become people capable of doing almost anything.

The workers at The Farm share one common trait. They were alone when the Boss Man picked them up and offered them a job. No one knew anyone else at the place. Every one of them started out alone. Any bonds they made they made after they started working at The Farm.

The work is hard and the days are long but no one complains much about that. They're worried about what would happen if they left The Farm. They're worried that the Boss Man won't let them leave no matter what he says. Two of them had tried but they were tracked down before they could get to a town or far enough that they weren't worth tracking.

They came back with the same story:

They're locked up in isolation in a large shed in back of the house, deprived of sleep and fed a broth with white bread three times a day. A counselor from the big house talks to them every waking hour of every day and night. Talks to them about how hard the world outside has become. Talks to them about how lucky they are to have food, shelter, clothing and someone who looks after them. After days and days of this, they can't tell exactly how long, they're weak and tired and too desperate to resist. They promise to be good workers. Loyal workers. True and honest and strong.

Only then does the Boss Man come in and tell them they can leave if they still feel the need. Only then does he tell them they're free. They don't believe him but they never try again. Life isn't that bad here. That much is true. In the slave days they'd whip you to the bone or cut a foot off so you can still work in the fields but you can't run.

Leon's problem is he's in love with a woman named Marge. She's the finest woman he's ever known (with the possible exception of his mother) and he would suffer all kinds of indignities just to stay in her company. That's wrong thinking of course. What a man or a woman for that matter will do for love is well chronicled but it can never ask you to give up your dignity and still be love. Leon knows it and he's a little ashamed he has to be reminded from time to time.

Marge's problem is she's in love with Leon. For weeks now, the two of them have wanted to join together as man and wife. The Boss Man won't allow couples or any other alliances that could end up turning against him. Leon's not really serious about leaving the place. He won't leave Marge and she's not ready to hit the road any time soon. He just likes to grovel about it and does so every night as his buddy Buck can attest.

We put all that to rest for the time being. This night belongs to celebration. They bring out some trail mix and canned fruits and make some hot chocolate that we all share. Someone even has a can of dog food that Cinnamon devours. They all agree that things are going to change starting in the morning and they invite me to stay around and witness it.

I decide to sleep on it and see what develops in the morning. I throw down my blankets and sleep until dawn. By the time Cinn rouses me the workers are already assembling for their morning meal. Buck comes over to invite me along. Maybe it doesn't seem like much but it's the best breakfast I ever had: fried veggies, hash brown potatoes and a slab of bacon. These are not things we take for granted anymore. Back at the Bridge Camp we have fresh fruits and vegetables we grow ourselves, along with a lot of oatmeal and trail mix, grains, nuts and dried fruits. Anything that keeps is at a premium and anything that doesn't is consumed immediately. I don't know where they get the meat. They don't raise pigs on the farm, or chickens or cows, so they must have traded for it.

I notice that some of the men and a few of the women are carrying hardwood walking sticks or lengths of pipe and someone is stationed outside the dining hall. There's a feeling of apprehension but nothing is said aloud. At least nothing I notice. What I don't know is that they're passing the word all day long about what they're going to do and the changes they're going to make.

Buck asks me if I can use a hammer and saw. I tell him I can and he invites me to work on the construction crew if I'm staying. I ask him what's going on and he tells me I'll see for myself if I hang around. He says they're not planning on confronting the Boss Man directly but they are going to make changes despite him. He gives me a wink and introduces me to the foreman of the crew, a stout man with a healthy gut and huge hands who goes by the name of Joe.

We go about our business, finishing up the shack and starting another when the chimes ring at the end of the workday. That's when I notice the first change. Leon grabs a few of his things and moves in with Marge. The two women who roomed with Marge move into the new shack and a couple of others shift as well.

They don't ask permission. They know it's against the rules and they're breaking the rules with their eyes wide open. They just do it and wait to see what happens next. Leon later relates that the Boss Man should have taken him out that first day. He knows he wants to but he's afraid the workers won't back him up. Leon is just as afraid they will.

People talk big but action is sketchy. It turns out the Boss Man is just as afraid his own thugs will back down. That's the trouble with hired help. They have no sense of loyalty. They have no pride. It's been that way all through history. Hired guns will turn and run the first time they come up against heavy resistance.

It's the same with Cinn and me. The workers don't ask if we can stay. They just invite us. We stay for another week or so and watch a number of changes happen. The workers take charge of the work assignments and talk about opening the books and sharing the profits – if there are any. The Boss Man makes the rounds, a couple of his thugs always in tow, but it's clear things have changed. He makes requests but he gives no orders. He just goes along with the program.

I decide I have all the story I'm going to get and a lot more than I expected. The day we say goodbye I swear I'll come back if it's humanly possible and Leon promises things will be better when I do. Once people get a taste of freedom they don't easily turn back. I have my doubts. The truth is we all do. But I have places to go, people to meet and stories to tell. That's what it was all about back then. Gathering stories from one group of people and taking them to another just to see what comes of it.

My head is teeming with thoughts. Have we already arrived at a place where ordinary people will give up their freedom? Is it worth it? When it comes down to it, the people have the power to overthrow their masters but they need some sense of order, sometimes they need an authority figure – especially now when the traditional authorities are no longer around.

Leon watches us go down the trail, a man and his dog, and he says a prayer. He's a religious man and he asks God so long as there is one to watch over us and keep us safe. Leon thinks the world of my dog. She's one of a kind. Like I always say, she's smarter than me. She would die to protect me and I'd do the same for her.

We build a small fire off the trail a good stretch from The Farm and sleep through most of the night. The last thing we want is to see the Boss Man again. I don't think he'll follow us but I'm not in the mood to take a chance. I am the unwitting catalyst to change so you never know when the desire for irrational revenge will overtake someone.

# HARD TIMES

When morning breaks we find a new trail, one that runs parallel to the road heading south, and we take it. We're back on the road going basically nowhere. As before the traffic is sparse but I notice a trend. The vehicles (mostly trucks and vans that can carry things) are getting older. I would later ask an auto mechanic about this. He told me someone with a sense of how things worked could repair the older vehicles. The newer vehicles require technological wizardry. No one is going to pay a hundred bucks to hook your car up to a machine so they can inform you that you need a part from a plant in China that no longer exists. The hybrids were popular for a while but once the battery runs dry there are no replacements.

We walk for a couple days, making camp by night well off the road, without encountering any trouble. On the third day a storm comes in and the air is noticeably crisper, marking the end of summer and the beginning of autumn. We seek refuge in an abandoned cottage maybe a hundred yards from the road. That's another trend. People are letting go of their homes in the country. It's too difficult to survive out here. It's better to band together in the towns and cities and share the burden.

We wait the storm out for two days before we get back out on the road. We turn down a ride from a man who's obviously drunk and looking for trouble. He's mad as hell but we just back off and walk the opposite way until he loses interest and drives on. A little later we take a ride from a couple in a blue van. They're dressed in jeans and work shirts, his plaid and hers khaki. They both have long hair tied back but that no longer carries any cultural meaning. Cutting hair has become an inconvenience that's often ignored. Most people carry a ragged look these days and no one pays it much attention.

They're heading for a place called Paradiso they had heard about in the foothills somewhere near Madera. It's squatters land and a group of college students and idealists are trying to create a sustainable and self-sufficient lifestyle with solar energy, innovative technology and environmentally conscious design. They aren't sure they have enough gas to get there but they're going to try. Gas is a problem even if you have money. It's rationed and the only gas stations left are controlled by the state. They're hard to find and generally dry three out of every four weeks. There are abandoned vehicles everywhere but almost all of them have been siphoned.

I tell them it's my intention to keep on moving but I wouldn't mind visiting the place to learn their story and pass it on to others.

His name is Holly, hers is Janis and they both think it's a great idea. They ask what I've learned so far. I tell them about the bridge camp and the farming cooperative. While I haven't come to any rock hard conclusions I'm leaning to the view that kindness and cooperation are the best means of surviving these times. Those who try to impose order or authority over large groups of people are fighting a losing battle. As long as the state is weak and unable to enforce its will, there's always a possibility that thugs and miscreants out for their own gain can take control. That isn't happening because the common decent people are banding together and figuring out how to make things work in a society without order. They're finding a way to establish their own kind of order based on kindness, charity and mutual respect.

I can see conflicting emotions in their expressions even as they nod and give encouraging remarks. I realize I'm expressing an optimism that's probably grounded more in hope than in fact. There are rumors of communities taken over by gangs, thugs and outlaws all over the state. Everything is uncertain. The future is a maze of possibilities and at least half of them are dark. How it all turns out nobody knows. Certainly not me.

We pass a few solar crawlers on the road – improvised vehicles with solar panels that crawl along in the daylight hours at anywhere from five to fifteen miles per hour. They are becoming more and more common and I figure it's because there are no longer any time pressures, no deadlines and no destinations that can't wait. That and of course the gas-rationing situation. Crawling along the road at a snail's pace on the power of the sun seems as good a way to pass the time as anything else.

We turn on a two-lane road heading east that becomes one lane, ragged with weeds and marked with potholes. We creep along like a crawler navigating around the potholes. People have taken to filling holes and repairing roads on their own but this road hasn't been tended to in a long while.

Janis notices a flag hanging limp on a windless day but there's something odd about it. As we draw near we see it's an old American peace flag but it's upside down. It's a sign of distress. We slow even more and discuss what it might mean. Holly suggests it could be a way of the keeping the riff raff out. Janis thinks it's a sign of distress and a warning. Combined with the state of the road, we decide it probably means the community has been hit with a serious sickness.

We pull over to discuss it further. Getting sick these days can easily cost your life. There's a shortage of drugs and medical supplies. The government passed a law requiring doctors and nurses to treat the ill and injured regardless of their ability to pay. It resulted in doctors and nurses going underground. Who could blame them? Once you start treating the needy it never ends.

Janis has some nursing experience and both she and Holly are determined to press forward but they won't ask me to go along against my will. I look at Cinnamon and tell them we're in. Whatever hardships lie ahead, I want to bear witness, help out if I can, and Cinn is sticking with me for better or worse.

We press on for another hour before we come to the place. There's a large octagonal structure with a sign reading "Paradiso" carved in wood over double doors. It's a community center where people can gather for meals and evening discussions. There are a handful of cottages surrounding a courtyard and a large windmill at its center. There are signs of other structures down walking paths outside our immediate view.

No one comes out to greet us. The place looks deserted. It's late in the day but the sun is still up. There should be plenty of activity to close a working day but there's nothing going on. The only sounds are crows feeding on vegetables in the community gardens. Something is definitely wrong.

Holly knocks on the door of the community center and knocks again. We hear no sign of activity on the other side of the door. We talk about going in and decide we will but Holly gives it one more try. He pounds it firmly like a police officer might do in former days. (If the police come to your door these days they have no intention of knocking.)

Just as we're going over our options, knocking the door down or finding another way inside, the door opens a crack and a woman with the saddest eyes I've ever seen and fatigue drawn in every movement of her hands and face peaks through.

"Can I help you?" she mumbles.

Holly explains why he and Janis have come. Janis adds that she has nursing experience and if anyone is sick she's willing to help. The woman squints and looks each of us over as if trying to decide what kind of people we are and what we intend. She signals someone inside before closing the door behind her and asking us to join her at a picnic table not far from where we stand.

Her name is Jo. She's in her late twenties but she looks much older with puffy yellowed eyes and what seems a greenish tint to her brown skin. She wears moccasins, loose fitting jeans and a cotton work shirt with a quilted shawl over her shoulders. We join her at the table and she tells us the story.

They had three visitors less than two months ago. They knew someone who knew about the place and they just wanted to see what was happening. After a couple days they moved on but they left the sickness behind them. One of them had a cough. He said he was recovering from a persistent cold and no one thought much of it at the time but within twenty-four hours several people were sick. Within forty-eight hours most of them were sick and within a week everyone was sick.

That was five weeks ago and things had only gone downhill. At this juncture only she and one other person are able to stand long enough to take care of the sick. While they still could they got word to the local authorities and someone from the Center for Infectious Diseases came out long enough to inform them that the illness was not tuberculosis, as they had feared; it was a persistent and resistant strand of a flu virus. Just another leftover from the lost civilization: antibiotics overuse causing killer viruses without cures or effective treatment. Antibiotics in kitchen cleaners, chickens, cows and turkeys, genetically modified organisms in farmed fish and every last rung on the food chain, what could go wrong? They left some aspirin and some medicines but there was little to no hope that they would work.

They were right about that. They didn't work. The only things they can do are the normal measures for the flu: try to keep the fever down, lots of fluids, cold compacts and lots of soup. After a week of suffering almost everyone tried to get up and help care for the others but they always fell back down.

There are only two people caring for twenty-nine others as we speak and both of them are feeling weak – too weak to go out and tend the garden, which they desperately need to survive not only the illness but the winter ahead.

If we stay, she confides, we will almost certainly get sick. She offers no assurances. No one has recovered yet and three have already died: a man, a woman and an infant child. They lay buried in shallow graves out back. The poor woman cries saying that she doesn't know what they will do with the next corpse. They don't have the strength even to drag the body out no less dig another hole in the ground. Despite all this, she says, if we stay they would be eternally grateful.

"If there is a God," she says, "God would be

grateful, too."

I admit I'm having doubts. A part of me figures I can use Cinn as an excuse. I can risk it myself but I cannot risk it for her. Holly and Janis are quick to offer their help in any way they can. They're staying and I decide I will stay as well. I'm a little relieved when Jo suggests that the three of us remain outside to tend the gardens, haul water from the well, and do whatever can be done without coming inside. The longer we remain healthy the better it is for everyone.

Jo offers us one more out, speaking with a reluctance that reveals the strength of her character. She tells us they have heard a rumor that this sickness never leaves the afflicted body. Some survive, the rumor goes, but they are always sick, always weak, and always struggling with the cough, the fever, the aches and pains. She coughs into a rag she holds in her hand and apologizes each time she does so.

"If I were you I would not stay."

Fair enough. We all understand. I figure Cinnamon understands better than I do. She stays away from the community room even when we approach it and she keeps her distance from Jo. She can smell the sickness, maybe even the death it promises. She wants me to know the danger she senses.

Jo quietly extends her hand down low and Cinn comes to her as if she holds an irresistible charm. She rubs behind her ears with whispers of good girl as only dog lovers can.

"Dogs thank God cannot get this human disease."

She informs us that the cottages are empty and we can settle in there. She promises to bring some bread and a vegetable stew before nightfall and ambles back to the community room like an old woman too tired to say any more.

"If you decide to stay, we'll work things out in the morning."

Janis volunteers to help with the evening meal but Jo throws up her hand. She's already explained that we can only help if we remain healthy and we can only remain healthy if we stay out of direct contact with the sick.

We huddle together like lost souls until Jo comes back out with a tray of food along with everything we need: silverware, bowls, bread and honey, a covered pot of stew, salt and pepper, plastic glasses and a pitcher of tea. She brings a can of dog food and a bowl for Cinn. She's as kind as an only child's grandmother yet she's clearly sick and tired. Her smile comes easy but she cannot sustain it. She asks if we need anything else and, when we defer with our thanks, she quietly returns to her duties, caring for those more ill than herself.

It's a virtual feast – even better than breakfast at The Farm and as good as any I can remember since hard times invaded our lives. The bread is fresh and home baked. The stew is delicately seasoned and full of fresh vegetables: potatoes, carrots, cabbage, broccoli, sweet corn and radishes, all grown in the gardens and a greenhouse out back. The tea is sweetened with honey. We eat everything set before us and Holly wonders aloud if Jo is trying to entice us to stay.

We talk until the sun goes down, leaving us in the light of a half moon, until we're too exhausted to carry on. Holly and Janis are more determined than ever to make this place work. They will make their stand here no matter the cost.

I reflect that this is what it all comes down to:

Choosing where to make your stand. Who do you want to stand with and what do you want to say? These people have a clear message and a purpose. They want the world to know there is a better way. I would love to stand with them but I know it's not possible. I have my family and I need to be with them if it comes down to that.

Janis and Holly choose the nearest cottage while Cinn and I choose a place across the courtyard, mindful that a couple needs privacy and space. The cottage has a thin layer of dust but it's otherwise clean. It's basically one room with a bed, a table and desk, and a small bathroom with a sink and toilet. There's a hot pan, a coffee maker and a row of shelves full of books. There's a lamp, an overhead light and a small room heater. We would learn that their electricity runs on solar arrays mounted on the roofs of each structure and an additional array out back. There are a handful of oil-powered generators for backup.

The bed is soft and comfortable with two pillows, a thick warm quilt and a stack of blankets in the closet. I settle on the bed with a copy of Cormac McCarthy's *The Road* and Cinnamon snuggles close for warmth.

I keep thinking what a beautiful place this really is: Open land with groves of valley oak, plenty of green plant life and fertile soil before the land turns hard and rocky in the foothills to the east. This land had given itself to growing fruits, nuts and vegetables for as long as anyone can recall. It's an ideal place for a group of like-minded people to come together and create a fruitful and sustainable life.

It requires a special breed of people who can bridge the gap between intellectual curiosity and the realities of surviving on and by the land. They need a deep understanding of human nature and a willingness to work hard and struggle and suffer disappointments and keep on working.

McCarthy's story as only he can tell it is grave and relentless. Humanity is stripped of its human values down to the level of rank survival. A man and his son roam the barren landscape of ruins searching for food and drinkable water. The social order is gone and what remains is ugly: violence without remorse, killing and cannibalism. I wonder if we will ever reach that place and if so how long it will take. I wonder if I even want to survive to live in such despair. Then just like McCarthy's nameless hero I remember my child, my children, and I know I will live as long as I can and suffer any misfortune or indignity to do whatever I can to help my kids. I have to survive out here if only to get back home. Still, I understand why the man's wife checked out and why she might have wanted to take her child with her. I suppose it's a matter of faith: If you believe in another world, an existence after this life, then it has to be better than this. My faith is just not that strong. I can't count on another world so I'll do the best I can in this world.

We awake in the early morning and go outside to find no one waiting. We explore the surroundings with Cinn taking the lead. There's a creek nearby running along the east side of the compound. There are gardens on three sides and an orchard of almond, cherry, olive and apple trees. There's a tool shed and storage directly behind the community building and a large greenhouse next to it.

It's clear they had planned every detail of the community in advance. Everything has a purpose and each element of the plan is placed and plotted for maximum efficiency. These are not hippies with a utopian dream of free love and worshiping unseen forces through psychotropic drugs. There are many earth based tribal communities springing up in the country. I hear about them from time to time and even thought about joining one but this place is different. These are serious people given to serious thought. The courtyard is an outdoor gathering place and the community building will serve the same purpose during the winter months or rainy seasons.

I pick apples, almonds and olives along the way, eating some and placing some in an old potato sack I've found, enjoying the fruit of other people's labor. When we finally wander back to the courtyard Holly and Janis are waiting for us along with Jo's partner in caretaking.

His name is Zar, short for Balthazar (although Jo would tell us she thought it was short for Zarathustra; Zar had been a philosophy student deep into Nietzsche but he wanted to leave all that behind). He explains that most of the original group were students at the University of California at Davis when everything went to hell. They lost their funding and could no longer sustain the student life so they banded together to form the community of their dreams, a paradise of sorts, a sustainable lifestyle, a life that leaves the earth unharmed yet fosters all the genuine pleasures of human existence: arts, crafts, science, intellectual pursuit, knowledge, communications. They want it all.

It seemed like a good idea at the time and maybe it was but then the sickness consumed them. Every hour of every day comes down to surviving now. Zar wants to talk. He wants to talk about philosophy, idealism, values, art and literature. He wants to talk about science or baseball or the weather – anything but what is happening here and now. He wants to talk like people used to talk before everything changed, before the sickness, but it isn't possible. People are depending on him just as they are depending on us.

"We're grateful you're here," he says. "And we hope you'll stay but we'll understand if you don't. This isn't your fight."

But it is our fight. It's everyone's fight now and more than ever each of us understands that we cannot run away.

Right now the future seems dark and frightening and it is precisely now that we must continue to imagine other worlds and then plot ways to get there.

Laurie Penny
*Utopia Now*

# THE UTOPIANS

They were students at the university when hard times came crashing down like the wrath of an angry God. Jo had a grant from the state for graduate work in engineering. Naturally, that was one of the first cuts from the state budget. Who needs engineers?

Zar survived on a combination of work-study and parental assistance in his senior year as a student of philosophy. Both came to a sudden halt. Times were hard and no one was spared. His parents said it was heart breaking but they didn't have enough saved to pay the mortgage, the medical bills and college expenses. The entire world was crumbling around them so Zar didn't have it in him raise his voice in protest. The truth is it was an easy decision and one that he would have made if they had not.

He was resigned to pack it in and go back home when Jo and her circle of friends came up with the idea of creating their own community. For Zar it was perfect timing. He was disenchanted with postmodern deconstructionism. He resented what he perceived as the growing religious nature of his discipline. He saw the irony of canonizing a man whose philosophy was antithesis to canonization. Friedrich Nietzsche was a great man with an exceptional mind but he was explicitly not a god. He was the philosopher who sought no followers yet attracted them in legions long after his death. Zar believed in the philosophy of Nietzche's fictional Zarathustra who instructed all to follow their own paths. It was a revelation that led him to profound and persistent doubt. When hard times came he was not only compelled to abandon his formal education, he was mentally primed to do so.

In some ways Zar is the least likely to join a community of idealists. He is certainly the least valuable. He has acquired no practical skills. He can pound a hammer if it comes to that but the others can design systems, energy systems and water systems, greenhouses and gardens. They possess the necessary skills to build a community from the ground up while Zar can only reflect on their work. He was hopeful he could acquire a serviceable skill but he was invited only because of his association with Jo and he knows it.

Jo is the epitome of useful. She was a valued member of a study group that was at the forefront of solar technology and solar technology is at the center of their community.

The core group consists of practical engineers but they are socially conscious enough to want couples. Contented couples mean less tension and greater focus on the task of building a self-sufficient community. They are less interested in utopian ideals than they are in utilitarian values. They possess the practical technological knowledge to create a working system unless human conflicts get in the way. Some of them believed a philosophy major would be useful in that regard and Jo sealed the deal. She would only join them if Zar went with her.

Even though his life had no particular direction he would not have been interested in forming a semi-utopian survivalist commune if not for Jo. Jo is a rock. When everything else is rusting away and collapsing like sand castles at high tide, Jo holds steady. Her belief system is firmly grounded in science but she also has an unbreakable spirit like the irrepressible star of that ancient musical *The Unsinkable Molly Brown*. No matter how bad things get she holds on to the belief that everything will turn out fine if we just keep moving, working and fighting. Jo believes in what they are doing and Zar believes in her.

They sent out the word to other universities while the web was still up and running. They had a location scouted out and plans were in place. They invited others of like interests and unique skill sets to join them. They recruited a few professors to back the project. One managed to get funding before the financial system broke down. He pilfered as much as he could from the university. Anticipating the fall of the Internet they downloaded and printed out everything they thought would be useful. They collected books and journals and technical papers. They shipped supplies down to the site in phases, one truckload after another, until they were ready to set up camp. It was a fairly remote location with a natural clearing by a creek and good fertile soil. With everything else that was going on, the locals didn't seem to mind a bunch of college kids and hippie types moving into the neighborhood.

They set up tents in the spring, planted a garden and started building the community center with a large kitchen and gathering hall. There were about two dozen of them in the beginning and others joined as they went along. They invited those who were useful to stay and encouraged those who were not to move on. Only a couple of times did they have to insist:

One was that special breed of troublemaker who wants to impose his leadership while another was just plain lazy. They came to their decisions as a group and confronted the offenders straightforward. The lazy guy packed his bag and left without a word the next day. The troublemaker resisted but after three days of being ostracized he gave a rant about the group's self-righteousness, their lack of vision and of course their lack of leadership. He left with a prophecy of doom and a curse of infernal darkness. They laughed about it at the time but when the virus came and knocked them all to their knees they remembered. You can't help wondering about a thing like that. Hardship is the fertile soil of superstition and desperation is the seed.

Before spring let out they finished the community center and kitchen. They expanded the garden, set up a greenhouse, finished building a warehouse for canning, drying and storage, started an expanded tool shop and began work on two rows of cottages. It was hard work but the payoff was phenomenal. It's amazing what people can accomplish when they know what they're doing and do it right. They worked from morning until dark with a couple of breaks for food. In the evenings after dinner they got out their instruments – mostly guitars and drums – and played until they were too tired to carry on. Most nights it didn't take long. Honest labor leads to deep sleep and engaging dreams.

While the weather was still moderate most of them slept in the courtyard under the stars but they all set up inside the community center. Each couple has a large wooden chest for their belongings and a rug that gives definition to their personal spaces. They have solar lights and plenty of energy to run the kitchen from the solar panels and the windmill in the center of the courtyard. They had a crew working on tapping the creek for waterpower as well. To an academic intellectual like Zar it was extraordinary. In a very short time a fully functional, self-sufficient working community emerged from the naked earth. It was a phenomenon he had not before witnessed and it seemed something akin to miraculous. This is how religions are born he reflected: an inability to explain phenomena in practical terms.

Midway through the summer they felt like they could relax. They had a good supply of dried goods, canned fruits and vegetables. They completed a second greenhouse and finished off enough cottages for everyone in residence and a couple of guests. They had three working solar crawlers that they sent up and down the valley to establish communications, gather information and set up an alliance of communities for trade and support.

They call their community *Paradiso* and from my perspective it's aptly named. They may not have set out to create a utopian society but what they accomplished is close enough. Everyone who's a part of it feels a sense of pride and belonging.

They were feeling strong and confident – maybe a little too confident. That's when the sickness hit. It hit hard and fast and it spared no one. They were all sick but some were sicker than others. Some people were coughing so hard they spit up blood. Reports came in from all over the valley. Everywhere you went people were getting sick. There was nothing they could do. They didn't have enough people and even if they had they didn't have medicines.

After another week of tending to people in their cottages, they moved everyone into the community center. It was the only way they could tend to them all. They lost three people in those first horrible weeks: an older man who was wise and prophetic named Raven, a wonderful and idealistic young woman named Breeze and a beautiful baby called Joy. Zar and Jo still mourn their passing.

After no one knows how many weeks (time becomes a relative value under constant pressure) it came down to Zar and Jo and Zar was fading fast. That's when we showed up. They still can't believe that anyone would come to their aid. No one had visited since the man from the Center for Infectious Diseases. They didn't know he put up a distress sign down the road. We're in virtual quarantine and anyone who gets close enough can see and smell a cloud of disease and a promise of death surrounding the place.

But here we were, knocking at the door and offering to help. Jo and Zar talked about how much they should tell us but in the end they could only tell the truth. They were a broken community preparing for the end. For the first week or so they were shocked every morning to find we were still here. A weight lifted. It felt like a physical force pushing down hard on their shoulders every minute of every day but it became lighter and easier when we stayed on to help.

It's constant misery. We can see, feel and smell death (it's gray and rotting) and watch it edging closer every day. They make a big pot of soup and spend most of the day moving from person to person, trying to get people to eat, putting fresh cold rags on their foreheads, wiping the sweat from their bodies, changing sheets whenever they can no longer stand the smell. Misery. Pure misery. There are times we are certain everyone is going to die.

Zar's bones and muscles ache, his head throbs and his cough sends him into a panic. He's afraid to lie down for worry that he will never get up again. He's so tired he doesn't know how he makes it from step to step.

It's nearly as bad for Jo but she never complains. They have to keep working and Jo will not give in. Someone has to tend the gardens, gather vegetables for the soup, and make sure the irrigation system doesn't break down. She keeps going and she keeps Zar going just watching her.

No matter how many times we repeat our assurances the doubt remains for a long time. It's just too much to ask of outsiders. It's too much to believe that someone in this bold new world would sacrifice their own interests, their own chances of survival, to help people they don't know and never had known. Maybe they're protecting themselves from unrealistic expectations. It's hard enough to keep your spirits up from day to day through the drudgery and struggle, never knowing if the sickness will once again knock you to your knees. Maybe they were protecting themselves from the possibility that their visitors would also be stricken. If we're all going to die anyway they don't want the deaths of three more on their shoulders.

They probably would not have pulled through if we hadn't shown up when we did. It's hard enough to believe that Zar and Jo kept going as long as they had.

If help hadn't come along the entire community and everyone in it would likely have succumbed. They would have died in their sleep, isolated and starving. They would have been just another tragic tale of the endemic flu that swept through the valley in hard times.

Holly, Janis and I tend the gardens, collect fresh fruits and vegetables, do the necessary maintenance and make sure everything stays in working order. When the weather starts turning colder we chop wood in preparation for winter. Zar and Jo share meals with us three times a day and spend the rest of their time inside cooking or tending the sick. They savor their time outside.

Janis pleads with them to let her inside. In what becomes a daily ritual Zar and Jo refuse to discuss it. They've made their decision. If it changes they will let her know. Until then we will all remain outside. Janis demurs as always but she inquires about the situation inside. They describe it as best they can. The sick are arranged in a circle on beds or cots or blankets and pillows around the periphery of an open space. The kitchen is separate and isolated by a doorway which they keep closed as much as possible. Janis asks about ventilation and they explain there's a fan to pump the air out in the ceiling. Janis suggests they open the doors as often as possible while the weather still permits and they agree to give it a try. From that point forward they open the doors in the morning, at noon and in the evening when they emerge to deliver meals and collect the fruits, vegetables, herbs and spices we've gathered during the day. It seems to help.

Zar jots down a list of chores that we build into a

routine. They pump water from the creek to the gardens, the greenhouse and the community building by means of wind and solar power. It's an automated system but it needs daily maintenance to check for and repair breakdowns and blockages. That becomes my primary duty. Janis and Holly spend most of their time in the gardens, weeding and repairing the wire fences that protect them from scavenging animals. The rest of the time we plant and tend plants in the greenhouse. We don't know how long the weather will hold but we will eventually depend on the greenhouse and the foods that are preserved in canning jars and stacked in a storage warehouse out back. We all spend time in the canning process as well.

We work the routine and the days go by almost unnoticed. As the weather turns we depend more and more on the backup generators but we do all we can to minimize their usage. There's an ample supply of candles and sometimes we spend time reforming the wax into new candles. We recycle everything from drinking water to sewage and we constantly work toward zero waste. We're growing a small crop of hemp to use for rope, twine, clothing and writing paper. For now we use the leftovers of society and dispose of them in the most earth friendly way we can. When the time comes we will be prepared. It's a workable plan.

With the cold coming on, we add woodcutting and stacking to our chores. As much as we want to avoid burning wood we have not been able to find an option that will keep us warm enough in the winter months. Instead, they've worked out a filtering system to minimize the damage. Anything else will have to wait until spring.

Holly is a very likable man and a good worker. I take a step back at first, listening more than talking, taking it all in. Zar and Jo both love my little dog and Cinn is growing attached to the place as dogs do. They love to run and explore but they're wired to find a home and root in. She loves Jo and Zar. It helps that they're the suppliers of food and treats but the affection is genuine and mutual. There were a couple of strays hanging around before the sickness but they wandered off in search of more reliable humans.

It's a week or two into our stay when the first of the sleepers awakens. That's what we call them: the sleepers. She's young and bright eyed despite the lingering effects of illness. Her name is Oleander. She had been a student of sociology before "the crash" as she calls it. She's genuinely overjoyed to see us. We connect her to the outside world. She wonders as they all do what's happening back home. Before the illness hit, they had participated in a communications project, a kind of pony express with bikes and motor scooters and solar crawlers instead of horses, but they had to drop out when they could no longer carry their weight. No one could. Social responsibilities are the first to fold when a crisis hits home. That much hasn't changed.

We tell her what we can, that times are hard everywhere, that people are finding all kinds of ways to adapt. We tell her this is the first place we encountered that was hit by the virus but there are rumors and stories that we can't confirm. It's something we all wonder. How widespread is it? Is it an epidemic? Has it hit others as hard as us? Some fear it's a kind of modern plague for which society, such as it is, is ill equipped to fight. Christian groups are loud in proclaiming the Apocalypse, the grand reckoning, the beginning of the end times. What else is new?

I relate my stories about the people I've met and the communities I've observed. I share my unfolding vision of pulling diverse communities together so that all can enjoy the best of each community. It goes beyond trading goods and services. It's an alliance of sharing, exchanging ideas, and people coming to a common understanding. I believe that any community that is isolated is in constant danger of dissolving either from within or without. I believe that the more communities we can bind together the stronger they will all be and the better our odds of survival.

They listen to my ideas but they remain skeptical. They like what they have going on here. They want to keep it like it is and they're afraid that outside influences will alter it in a bad way. They want to realize their own vision and believe their best chance is to keep Paradiso apart from the world. I argue that no community should be called upon to give up its independence or its uniqueness. It's as unnecessary as it is undesirable. Each community would mark its own path and the alliance would only help to ensure that each could survive.

We spend many hours talking things through, exploring the possibilities. More and more people are getting out of their beds now, recovering enough to stand and then walk and then join the group outside. Eventually I convince Zar that I'm right. If they were a part of a greater community this illness would not have threatened their very existence. They would have had help from the early stages. They will face other threats as time goes by and they will need help again. By the same reasoning, they have to be prepared to help others. It only makes sense.

# HARD TIMES

One of my ideas is to maintain the road that leads to Paradiso. I envision a constant traffic of solar crawlers traveling from the south as far as Fresno to the north as far as Chico. I envision a transport service, an exchange of information, goods and personnel. I figure each member community can accept responsibility for maintaining its share of the road, for building campsites and ensuring security. The more I talk about it the more I persuade those who listen. After a while they realize it's not just the fact that I'm enthusiastic; it's that I'm talking about the future—and not just the immediate future. I have a vision. I'm talking about a new order, a new way of living, a new and better society. It's been a long time since anyone talked in those terms. I guess that's why Paradiso (I call it the Sun Camp) so appeals to me. It's a place of dreams and a place that encourages dreamers. I'm a natural dreamer and it seems as though I've found a home. More than anywhere else I've encountered, I feel I belong here and I'm welcome.

My thoughts wander more and more back to my family, my wife and kids, always with the same fear. I run through the possibilities – sending a message, going back either to stay or to visit or just to observe – but I always come to the same conclusion: there's little I can do to help. Nothing has really changed. I can only get in the way. More harm than good. The time will come. Soon I hope. But it hasn't come yet. It's harder and harder to live with but nothing has fundamentally changed.

I go to sleep early with Cinn snuggled at my side and awaken in the darkened, early hours of the morning with a cold sweat covering my body. I struggle to get up and throw some water on my face but I lose the battle. The next thing I know I'm in the community room on the cot that Oleander once occupied. Suddenly, instead of caretaker I'm among the cared for. I will learn firsthand the horrors of this virus that creeps into your body and holds it for as long as it can until it releases you. One way or the other.

At first I fight back as everyone else does, following a stubborn and irrational instinct, refusing to believe that I've fallen victim. Again and again, as Jo or Zar try to talk me down, I try to get up but my body refuses. The pain is so acute and runs so deep that any movement triggers a cascade of agony. The fever takes hold of my mind so that I no longer know where I am or why or how I got here. Often as not, I can't remember who I am. At times I think I'm being held hostage by people who want to enslave me or steal the organs of my body. I'm being tortured. I'm being held against my will. I'm a soldier in the hands of an unknown enemy. They inject me with drugs that stop me from moving or thinking or trying to escape. They want answers but I have none. I cannot understand their questions.

The only thing that can bring me back to earth and reality is the worried gaze of my loyal friend and companion. Cinn is with me constantly. She lays her head and paws on my chest and I never doubt her purpose is to comfort and heal me. When the mind suffers it takes little comfort. It seizes it and casts it away. When the body suffers it seizes pain, pulls it in and holds it like a toxic treasure. She alone is my salvation and comfort. She alone can ward off the unseen demons attacking my mind and body even as I sleep, even as I run, even as I hide in the darkest corners of my subconscious mind.

# HARD TIMES

The sickness comes in waves, washing over me, drowning me, dragging me through a dark landscape with shadow creatures, yellow eyes and snarling, scowling lips, surrounding and devouring me. I'm blue flame hot and shivering cold. Then, just as I think I can bear no more it releases me, offering a glimpse of wellness before it resumes its punishing march.

My sickness takes a toll on everyone in the camp. They are already numbed by the deaths they have endured and the struggle they have overcome. I have become more than a friend. I'm someone they have come to respect. I'm part of their family. I am a brother. I never talked much about my own family before the sickness grabbed me. I told them who they are and where they are and why I left them but that's all. I'm afraid that if I talk about them too much it will consume me. I don't want to go back until things are better, until I can be sure that my presence will not add to their hardship. So I didn't talk about them. But now that I'm sick that's all I talk about. I fade in and out of consciousness and every time I awake I wonder where I am and I ask for Madge and Denim and Charlie. I demand to know where they are and if they're safe.

Oleander holds herself personally responsible for my illness. She believes she infected me. Whether that's true no one can say but she feels it. Sooner or later what you feel becomes the truth. She and Janis sit by my side around the clock and of course Cinn is there too. That little dog just lies by my side with her head on my chest looking at my face for signs of life or the shadow of death. When I wake up she licks my face and reminds me I'm loved.

They send someone on a solar crawler to check up on my family. They had a long discussion about

83

whether or not to tell my wife that I'm sick and might die. They decide not to tell her because they're afraid she would come to care for me and the sickness would take hold of her too. They don't want to leave our children orphans. They aren't sure if it's the right thing to do. In her place most people would want to know. Most of them would have wanted to know but it comes down to the children and that's what they decided. They just want to be able to tell me that my family is safe. If they aren't safe they will hold on to that knowledge until I'm fully recovered or until the end draws near. None of them had faced such decisions in their prior lives and nothing about it comes easy. It is the blessing and the curse of the times. We're not bound by the laws or the moral codes of the state, the nation or the media. We make our own laws and live with the consequences.

They faced the same decision regarding a professor from the university who came down to observe their progress and offer advice. She was close to Jo and a number of other students. Jo said that without Dr. Arakawa none of this would have happened. She was a brilliant physicist with practical knowledge in energy systems – particularly solar energy. She had a husband and two children who stayed behind in Davis. She was more than pleased with what they had accomplished but she came at exactly the wrong time.

It was the week the illness hit so no one knew how bad it would be. She held on for a long time. Like so many others it seemed she would recover. She was up and walking around in late autumn. But she had a relapse and it hit her hard. They had already informed her family that she was ill. They were frank about the seriousness of the illness though they were confident of her recovery chances at the time.

Her family came immediately. All of them. Jo and a friend tried to stop them at the gate down the road but they wouldn't listen. They even had the professor write a letter to dissuade them but it seemed to have the opposite effect. The father, a professor of sociology, tried to persuade his son and daughter to stay behind but they refused to hear it. They were a family. Their wife and mother was deathly ill and they would be there by her side just as she would if it was one of them. It's strange that intelligent and educated people, people who dedicate so much of their existence to reason, yield logic to emotion when it counts most. I can't say that I would do otherwise.

Dr. Arakawa held on until Christmas. The winter was mild but a storm came down from the mountains on Christmas Eve and held for three days. It snowed. The locals said it hadn't snowed here for twenty years. It was comforting. Like chicken soup or fresh baked bread. They stayed inside most of the time, sipping warm drinks and talking softly about everything that had happened and whether or not it was worth it.

When Dr. Arakawa died Christmas morning there was a deep sense of loss. They were gathered in the community room when the family came in and announced her passing. Her husband said she was coherent in the last moments before her death. She said that what we were doing was important. Her last wish was that we should carry on and complete the work that she had helped give birth. She said there would always be hardships but they would succeed as long as they refuse to fail. Those were her last words: Refuse to fail.

Her family returned to Davis and they hadn't heard

a word since. They could only hope and pray they hadn't contracted the sickness.

It's a solemn Christmas. Zar comes to see me around midnight. Oleander is asleep in a chair with an open book in her lap: McCarthy's *The Road*. He talks to me in soft tones for quite a while. He tells me what happened and how sorrow had a grip on the camp. He says they need me to pull through now more than ever or they might not make it. He explains how important the professor had been to everyone. He says he feels the same way about me and he thinks the others have the same feeling. He asks me to think about it and if I can find a way back to them I should. After that he just stands there looking at my face, wondering what I'm experiencing, wondering if it's selfish to ask me to think of others, thinking that somehow I understand what he's talking about. I do. Somewhere in my subconscious I hear every word and I understand.

I die a thousand agonizing deaths before I finally find my footing. When I do, Cinn is there, licking my face, welcoming me, and Janis is tending to me. Only a handful of people are still sick. The others have recovered and rejoined the outside world. When they're certain I'm well enough, I'm allowed to go outside as well. A few days later Jo tells me about the professor who died. The camp is in mourning and will remain so through the winter.

At one point Zar asks me what I remember when I was under the spell of sickness. Most of what I remember has no words. There were times when I felt warmth and a sense of closeness to those around me. I couldn't recall what was said but I knew how it felt. It felt like someone pulling me out of a hole, a deep dark hole. I felt gratitude. It gave me direction and fueled my will to fight back. I told him I remember what he said on Christmas, that I heard and understood though I was unable to respond.

Zar is deeply moved. He says he doesn't know if there is a God or another life after this one. On so many levels it doesn't make sense. But he feels strongly that I had gone somewhere else and made a choice to come back. He knows it's irrational. It goes against everything he's been taught by people wiser, more educated and smarter than himself. Still he's come to the conclusion that an individual has a choice even in death. Jo disagrees. If wishes and prayers could bring a person back from death they would have worked on Dr. Arakawa. She chooses to place her faith in science and her prayers are scientific inquiries. She is no less grateful that I survived but she refuses to attribute it to anything but loving care and the laws of probability.

It comes down to religion. No objective observer can doubt that religion is a mixed blessing at best and a scourge on humanity at worst. The problem with religion is orthodoxy. When people band together and recruit others on the condition that any knowledge that is not established in orthodox beliefs must be rejected it becomes the enemy of social and personal progress and growth. It becomes the enemy of science and a threat to social order. Jo and Zar agree that orthodox religion should have no part in their community but that all belief systems should be regarded with absolute tolerance as long as no one is harmed or hindered in any way. That is the unspoken creed of the Sun Camp.

I have missed Christmas but there's good news: my family is safe. They're struggling like everyone else but they're safe. That's all. They did not make contact and when they explain why, I agree. After all we've been through, it is not a risk I would have taken.

The air seems fresher, the sunlight brighter and the whole world seems a better place. I resolve to go home as soon as I'm able. We would work it out. For better or worse, we would find a way to work it out. It takes a while for Zar and Jo and Holly and the rest to persuade me that I should wait until spring when I'm fully recovered and the weather is more forgiving.

After Christmas the freeze lifts and a series of strong storms ride in on waves of fluctuating temperatures. Warm spells follow cold spells and when they meet, hailstorms, lightning and strong winds pound us. We spend much of our time making repairs. One of the worst storms brings down an ancient oak tree on top of the workshop. We all know the prophecies of the environmental movement concerning global warming and climate change and here's the proof – a little late but clear and powerful. The good side of economic collapse is that it closes down massive industries. The planet is in the process of cleaning up industrial poisons and toxic waste in the air, the water and in the land. The Sun Camp is determined to keep it that way.

That is in fact their prime directive: To live in harmony with the planet.

When I leave in the spring Zar decides to go with me. The Sun Camp is back in working order. They have a cottage industry producing more solar panels and crawlers than they can reasonably use. They have a mission to trade their technology and expertise for anything useful that other communities can bring to them. I have an idea that each community possesses something that they do better than anyone else. The Sun Camp does energy systems, The Farm does food, the Bridge Camp does masonry and brickwork and the neighborhood in town, while they have no particular specialty, has tools and supplies and machinery that others lack. Everyone can contribute in some unique way to the whole.

The first step is to clear the path and to get everyone to agree on the vision. I'm sure we can get the Bridge Camp and The Farm to buy in but I'm not so sure about the city people. I want to convince my immediate family to move to Paradiso. It's a delicate balance because I don't think my extended family – my mother-in-law, my Aunt Mildred and Uncle Bud, or Carlin and his family – are a good fit for Paradiso. Carlin is too bossy and set in his ways and the others are not physically able to contribute in a meaningful way. The time might come when the camp can accommodate a more diverse community, including the elderly, but at this stage they just aren't ready.

We're a little worried about security. The Sun Camp people have kept the road clear and made repairs and established campgrounds that can't be seen from the road but we're hearing reports of criminal gangs roaming from town to town, taking what they want or need and leaving them destroyed. The camp is worried enough to build a watchtower and there are plans for a security wall. We have come too far and built too much to risk letting a gang of thugs and criminals tear it down.

We travel light so we can get off the road and take cover if someone approaches. The gangs invariably use internal combustion vehicles so it's easy to hear them coming. Cinn sounds an alarm and after a couple of close calls she's learned to be quiet while we hide in the brush.

The rains of spring arrive and at times fall hard, slowing our progress. We have to clear the road of branches and debris and take cover to wait out the rain. On several occasions we hide from clusters of motorcyclists but we never really feel threatened. The off road camps are sanctuaries for people of like mind. They know of the Sun Camp and they've established a relationship even it's only for communications. One of the campers we encounter comes from my hometown and talks about a massacre that has taken place there.

A gang of released prisoners was wiped out by the military. No one from the community has been harmed but some of them, the story goes, had to be relocated when their homes were destroyed. There's no way of knowing whether it is my neighborhood but it worries me. We agree that I should get home as soon as possible so when we reach The Farm, Zar stays and I take the crawler. There are enough crawlers on the road now that Zar can easily catch a ride so we don't have to worry about him getting stranded. We're a little worried about me traveling alone but a man's got to do what he's got to do. I need to get home.

I introduce Zar to Leon and Madge and they take him in and welcome him as if he's one of their own. Their gardens and greenhouses are state of the art and their canning operation is professional. Leon is already convinced that solar is the way to go and Zar shares some of his ideas concerning wind and water energy. For the next three days he will talk to people with wide eyes, open minds and souls eager to engage.

The only problem of course is the Boss Man, a

leftover from the old school who resents any ideas that come from the workers no matter how much sense they make. Zar talks to him only briefly. He's intransigent as we figured he would be. It's a problem that will have to be overcome if we're going to make any headway at The Farm.

I press on with a purpose to make good time. I stop hiding and just move to the side of the road when others come by with their motorcycles and an occasional truck or van. None of them pay much attention to a man and his dog. It seems they're in a hurry to get wherever they're going as fast as they can.

I talk to one man on a scooter who has run out of gas. He doesn't know where he's going. Just that he's moving on. Like nearly everyone I encounter, the man has heard about the massacre but he doesn't know much about it. Only that it happened somewhere on the west side where my family resides. He seems a good and decent man so I give him directions to The Farm. There's a marker by the road, a small pyramid of rocks. I tell him it's ten miles off the road but he can expect help there and a good meal if he isn't afraid to work for it. I tell him to ask for Leon and tell him Stone sent him.

I move on more determined than ever to get home. It's a hard go battling the rain on a daily basis but on the day we reach the outskirts of town the skies are as clear as the waters of a virgin lake. I never thought the sight of that old bridge with its guardian lions would fill my heart with such joy and I realize we have one more stop to make. Whatever fate has in store for us down the road it will have to wait an hour or two while I visit an old friend.

I find Sugar working in a clearing on the far side of the bridge, building a village that can accommodate a growing community. If not for Cinn prancing up to give him a good pawing and a lick in the face, Sugar might not have recognized the man approaching him. I guess I'm a sight to see. I probably look ten years older with long hair and a full beard. My clothes are ragged but clean. My belly is full and my eyes shine with wonder.

He marvels at the crawler I'm driving, by far the nicest he's seen and fully stocked with plenty of food and supplies. We embrace as old friends and I explain I'm on my way to my family's house but I feel obliged to stop by and say hello.

He can't add much about the massacre except that it happened and if it wasn't my neighborhood it was close to it. Everyone in town heard the explosion of gunfire. It sounded like a war zone. Then it went quiet. The word is the only people who died there were the criminals and they died by the dozens.

I nod and we share a moment of heavy silence. Sugar says a little prayer. Then we walk back to the bridge, sit down like old times and share our stories. There's some good and bad in both. The bad for me of course is that I almost died of the sickness that swept through the valley like a plague. Every community lost someone. The Bridge Camp lost more than its share. It's always worse when you lose the younger ones and that they did. Sugar said it made them stronger though. It made them get serious about building their own little village out there in the clearing. They need shelter from the storm – more than a bridge can offer – and they have plenty of good working people with the skills to build it.

When the heavy rains came it added a sense of urgency to their work. The river is rising. It had already crowded out some of their people down by the riverbank. The word came down from the north that the levees up there had failed. All those new towns built on the flood plains with cheap money from crooked bankers and brokers were flooded out and the people who still lived there had no place to go. They had already seen the first trickle of a great migration yet to come. More and more people would be looking for shelter anywhere they could find it. The Bridge Camp intended to do its part.

The good news of course is the fact that I survived and met some really good people along the way. I tell him about the farming operation not far down the road and the troubles they've had with their boss. The place supplies much of the city with fruits and vegetables to keep people from starving, including the Bridge Camp. They have their gardens and greenhouses up and working by now and they don't take any more than they need but they're grateful for what they gave when they needed it most.

I'm proud of the farm workers for standing up to their boss and asserting their rights. Sugar gives me a little advice in that regard. It seems to him property rights don't hold for much in this new world and no man has a right to profit from desperate times like this Boss Man was doing. But seeing as he had a deal with the authorities to provide food to the city, the workers had to be careful. The cops and the military don't answer to much these days but if they think their food supply is threatened they just might come down with the hammer of vengeance.

I wonder if it might do some good to talk to the

authorities myself. Sugar encourages me to do just that. He tells me it can't do any harm and it might just set their minds at ease.

Mostly I talk about the place they call Paradiso – a little Paradise. I call it the Sun Camp due to the fact that they use the power of the sun for energy. I tell him about all the things they've accomplished, including solar panels and solar vehicles better than anyone else's. It began as a community of college kids and wide-eyed idealists but developed into a promising model for a new social system.

I believe they're well on their way to building a fully self-sufficient community that does no harm to the land they live on, the water they drink or the air they breathe. Sugar tells me the Bridge Camp has pretty much the same idea but it's a little further down the road. Survival is still the paramount concern. Until people begin to feel secure about making it through the day they will never think about tomorrow. Some like Sugar think ahead and make plans but most are still trapped in the day to day. It's a struggle but he continues to work on it. He says it's like building a great tower. You have to lay out the groundwork first. The new camp with sturdy brick and mortar housing down in the fields is a good beginning. It starts the people thinking. Soon they'll be able to dream.

Sugar senses that the Sun Camp is where I eventually wanted to settle. I sound him out about living there too. He seems to feel good about that but he's already decided the bridge is his place to make a stand. He's planted like an old oak tree and the only way to move him out is to cut him down or blow him over with a strong wind.

He arrived under the bridge a man without family

and he became a part of a community, well liked and respected. The Bridge Camp *is* his family now. At least that's how he feels about it. Maybe the time will come when he feels that old familiar itch to move on but that time is still a long ways down the road or so it seems as he looks over the day's work.

He says he'd be pleased to visit wherever I end up, the Sun Camp or anywhere else, and he's willing to help any way he can. Then he tells me about the plans they have for their village, shows me some of their drawings and blueprints so I can see they're serious, and takes me on a little tour. They have most of the walls up for a full-sized community center shaped like a U around a big courtyard. They have several masons in camp and they're building out of bricks they formed from riverbank clay and straw. I'm amazed at what they're doing and offer the idea that they can trade with The Farm and the Sun Camp in such a way that everyone would be better off. Sugar likes that idea and goes to work talking it up with the others that very evening. The crawler I'm driving is a good way of selling the idea of solar energy. It seems everyone who sees it can't believe how sound and practical it is. Before the crash we were all taught to believe in the limitations of solar and other forms of renewable energy. The kids at the Sun Camp came at it with the opposite expectation. They believed in the potential and worked to expand it.

Trade with other communities is something the Bridge Camp has never gotten around to considering. It never came up. Maybe it should have but it didn't. Because they were the Bridge Camp, full of vagabonds, bums and outcasts, people thought they didn't have much to give. It only shows how much people don't know. The most valuable things you have are not things at all. In this world things like gold and silver and precious stones don't amount to much. Not like food and water and a safe place to lay your head. But the most valuable thing people possess is knowledge. Like Sugar always says, it doesn't matter what you look like or where you're from or how much coin you have in your pocket, it's what you know that counts.

The Bridge Camp is a goldmine with people who know how to build things and get things done. They have engineers and carpenters and woodworkers and well drillers and mechanics and plumbers and ditch diggers and anything else you might need to build a community. But most of all they have a working knowledge of masonry and they make some good strong bricks that will stand up to the worst storms. They have developed some first class roofing panels as well.

I take a fresh look at my friend and notice for the first time that his clothes are a bit ragged and frayed. I look at myself and note the same pattern, worn thin at the elbows and knees. Sugar reads my mind and laughs: *Yep, just a couple of bums sitting under a bridge.*

I laugh with him and share the thought that jumps into my head. I figure at least half the homes in Grace's neighborhood probably still have sewing machines, some of them the old mechanical kind. The people at the Sun Camp are growing hemp with the thought that it could be used for anything from rope and twine to baskets and watertight containers to sandals and clothing. With a little planning and organization the old neighborhood could start up a cottage industry in clothing and clothing repair.

Sugar nods and agrees it's great idea. Everyone has

something to offer.

We shake hands and I move on, anxious to see my family. I leave behind the seeds that I hope will take root and grow into something we can all take pride in. We're no longer just surviving day by day. We're building for a future.

I wanted to change the world. But I have found that the only thing one can be sure of changing is oneself.

Aldous Huxley
*Point Counter Point*

## THE NEIGHBORHOOD

There's an old song that says: You don't know what you've got till it's gone. We never realized how true that was until hard times came to our house. We had a good life though we may not have fully appreciated it at the time. We had what you're supposed to want: two kids and a home in a good neighborhood with a good school. We had everything we needed and anything we wanted we could get if we set our minds to it. We were content and secure. We never dreamed it could happen to us.

All those people who told us after the fact that we were dreaming, living beyond our means, taking too many risks, where are they now? Is it our fault everything went to hell? No. It's no one's fault. It's everyone's fault. It's the banks and the realtors and the greedy moneychangers on Wall Street. It's the corrupt politicians and the people who voted them into office. No matter who takes the blame, it hit us like Katrina hit New Orleans back in the day. Maybe we should have known better. Maybe we should have been more cautious but, really, it would only have delayed the inevitable. It's a sinking ship and the righteous go down with the rest of us.

It's easy to get lost in self-pity. Taking the blame becomes a power play. If only I'd made better decisions, if only I'd done something different at a critical time, things would have been better. The truth is there isn't a damn thing I or anyone else could have done. The deck was stacked. And here we are.

It's hard times for everyone but it's particularly hard for a man like Carlin. He fought as hard as he could for as long as he could to save their home and the life they had built. His story is my story and our story is the same as millions of others. He had a good job supplying tools and parts to American factories before American industry was exported to Mexico, India, China, Malaysia or whatever third world country provided the cheapest labor. He picked up work wherever he could find it but it was never enough. No one can support a family on what they pay you for flipping burgers or stocking shelves at the grocery store. There just wasn't anything else for him. He tried. He gave it everything he had. No one was as sorry as Carlin when he came up short. He's a military man and he's very proud.

He believes everyone blames him for everything that happened. Not the financial crisis, not the total breakdown in social order, but for what happened with me and Madge and the family. The house just wasn't big enough for two grown men so I left. Carlin in his deluded mind thinks everyone holds him responsible for pushing me out the door. He never asked me to go. He never wanted me to go. He probably never gave it more than a passing thought. But he still thinks the family blames him and he resents it. There are times when he lets down his guard and lets his rage come spewing out: Anyone can play the blame game and he took his turn. Where was I when the tornados hit and they had to make repairs? Where was I when the virus came through and they had to set up roadblocks and impose quarantine? Where was I when the gangsters came and shook them down for food? Maybe the family should blame me for not being around when all the shit went down.

In the world of his own creation, someone has to take the lead so he stepped up. When there wasn't enough space they added a room. They needed a greenhouse so he took the initiative. If I resented his leadership I never said a word. Still, he feels certain that everyone blames him and he carries that on his shoulders with every step he takes.

What was difficult before became all but impossible when Uncle Bud and Aunt Mildred moved in. What else could they do? They had no place else to go. Carlin would have turned them away. He said it would have been hard but someone had to make the hard decisions. Too many hands on board, too much dead weight, you do what you have to do.

The trouble is it wasn't Carlin's decision to make. It was Grace's house and it was her decision. She has a soft heart so everyone knew she could never turn them away. They were family. In her mind that was all there was to it.

Carlin sees it differently. He wanted a family vote. Madge said fine if you let Bud and Mildred vote. Even Carlin's wife Joan sided with the rest of us. Carlin said he wouldn't put them on the street. He'd find them someplace to live. Madge said there was no place to live. I got a little red in the face and said it was Grace's call and that was the end of it. And so it was.

Grace was never the kind to look back in life. Even

as she grows old she prides herself in looking ahead. When hard times came for the second time in her life, however, she discovered her mind traveling to the past, seeking refuge in better days. She never thought she'd outlive her husband. Bill was strong and she was less so. He was hardly ever sick and she often was. Growing up they had both known hard times. They were the children of refugees, uprooted from their Oklahoma homes and dropped in the great central valley of California where there were no jobs waiting. They knew what it was like to go to bed hungry. They knew what it was like never to buy new clothes. They grew up knowing what hard times meant but their children had no idea.

When we first came to live in Grace's house we thought it was as much for her as for us. Maybe we were just fooling ourselves. We could not understand how an old woman who spent the bulk of her life in the company of others might want to be alone. Grace suspected many old people felt as she did but their children cajole them into giving up their solitude for the security of having someone there to call the hospital if something unfortunate should happen - like falling and not being able to get up. There comes a time of course when that may become necessary and more often than not they end up in a rest home, hardly ever their children's homes. A rest home is the last place Grace would want to rest - especially if it was her final stop.

But she welcomed us into her home recognizing that what was happening in the world had happened before when she was a child. She was neither surprised when Madge's family was followed by Carlin's family nor when Uncle Bud showed up with that "drunken harlot" of a wife Mildred. Grace tried not to judge but sometimes they make it so obvious. Uncle Bud is harmless enough and often amusing; he's just a waste of space. Mildred is something less than that – a waste of good alcohol is what Grace thought but she would never say it aloud.

She just took them all in without complaint. She took them in and shared what she had just as relatives and friends had taken others in when their time of need arrived. It was hard times and everyone had to look out for one another. Hard times make the family grow stronger if it doesn't break them apart. It made them stronger during the Great Depression and it would make us stronger today.

She sought solitude in her room and considered it being thoughtful until Madge told her the family was concerned. She thought Grace was spending too much time alone. She thought it meant she was unhappy. Grace tried to tell her that her happiness really wasn't the family's concern. Sometimes she enjoyed happiness and other times she enjoyed solemnity. It was not a concept they could wrap their minds around so she ultimately relented and spent more time around the others.

She eventually grew to appreciate the children, even the spoiled little ones that her daughter-in-law Joan created like Frankenstein's monster. Like a pet dog there is no such thing as a bad child, only a poorly reared one. In the traditional roles, grandmothers are supposed to be the spoilers of the family. In the new world, where grandmother and children are constant company, Grace sometimes has to assume the parental role of disciplinarian. It is not a role she relishes but she feels someone has to do it. Children do need guidance.

Carlin took a long time getting over the decision to let Bud and Mildred move in. Like a child, he had to get his way and he carried a grudge as long as it would let him. If you ask anyone else, he's the one who plays the blame game. Blame it on compassion. Blame it on the moon. Blame it on Grace or Madge or me. Anyone but him. He says he just wants to do the right thing. He just wants what's best for the kids. That's the way he looks at it.

Looking back, that was when I changed. I had always had hope. Even when things were falling down all around me I had hope. I never give up and I always try to have encouraging words.

"Don't worry, babe, we'll make it work."

When I left Madge was shattered. She shared the note I had written with Grace and Grace's heart went out to both of us. In her eyes, I'm a good man who has earned her love and respect. I work hard. I put the needs of my wife and children before myself. She understands how hard it must have been and how I must have felt when I made the decision to leave. Right or wrong, she knows I did it for them.

That is what hard times do to us. They make us confront choices we should never have to make.

Madge was so angry she could hardly think. She felt abandoned at a time of need. She blamed me for abandoning the children. Nothing could have been further from the truth. I gave up everything I treasured. I gave up my place in the home and my share of the family's food to help them all.

As time went by Madge began to understand. I took a look around and said: I take more than I give. It sounds unkind but at the time it was true. The family was better off without me. They had more food at the end of the month. They didn't really need me. Everyone knows I love Madge and I love those kids more than I love myself. It took all the courage I had for me to leave and most of the family – the adults at least – respect my decision. The kids need more time.

Madge would never forget the day she came home with two bags of groceries worried that they would not have enough to last the month. It was a familiar dilemma: whether to buy more macaroni and cheese products that lacked nutritional value but are cheap enough to last or try to ration more nutritional foods. With sporadic electricity fresh fruits, vegetables and meat would go bad within a week or two. The garden we planted in the back yard never produced enough. Nuts and grains are best but it's difficult to get the children to eat enough of them and the price keeps going up while the rations go down.

It was a constant struggle but at least it gave her an opportunity to think about something other than the problems we were having trying to live together: too many people and not enough room. Carlin and I were having male competition troubles. The kids were constantly fighting, yelling, screaming. In normal times it would have all washed over. Kids are kids and men are men. But these are not normal times. Two families, an elderly couple and an elderly woman in a small two-bedroom house made for relentless pressure.

Madge began to quarrel with Carlin's wife. Joan was the kind of woman who thought it her duty to stand up for her own regardless of right and wrong. No one seemed to realize that we would all have to make adjustments and we were not alone. Everyone has to make adjustments.

Joan's idea of parenting is a low-pitched drone. She was on her little boy Nathan and her little girl Shannon all the time but if anyone else admonished them in any way she went on the defensive. No, she went on the attack. Things got so bad that Grace withdrew to her small room, a converted study, for most of the day. Carlin refused to intervene and I wanted nothing to do with it.

That was what Madge came home to that day. She put away the groceries, checked on the kids playing outside, and went to our bedroom where she found my note. She read it three times before it registered and then she began to cry.

She cried for a long time and then, when her tears were all spent, she got angry. A father does not abandon his children under any circumstances. They needed me. They needed me now more than ever. I could offer all the excuses in the world but it couldn't erase the fact that it was selfish. I was looking after myself. What kind of a man was I? Had she been fooled all these years?

No, she thought, I was a good man. I was doing what I thought was right. But she needed her anger to make it through the days. Isn't it strange what we need? No matter how unreasonable we hold on to it when there's nothing else. We hold on to it until we find something else to hold on to or we go insane. Sometimes we need to hold on to our anger. Like Madge did.

She too needed someone to blame and I was her someone. She spent the next month in a constant rage, railing at the kids, arguing with Joan, pleading with her mother to stand up to them, stirring up trouble and looking for it. By all accounts it was horrible. She was becoming someone she didn't know and didn't like. She read my letter every night as if it hid some secret, as if she could change the meaning by discovering the code but of course she couldn't.

It was her job in those days to take the kids to school and she held to it as if it was all that mattered. Kids have to have an education. At least that's what we were taught. You have to have a good education to get a good job, to secure your future, to become a good and useful human being. It never occurred to her back then that the future might not be the kind of place where a traditional education still mattered.

She still believed in the old ways and the old values so every day she got the kids up at half past six, got some food in them and marched them off to Johansen Elementary. The schools fought hard to stay open. Even after the money ran out they stayed open. Even after the janitors and cafeteria workers left they stayed open. They lost the vice principles and deans and the specialists and they stayed open. The teachers lost their pay and they hung on as long as they could. The parents took up collections and struggled on but in the end it was a losing battle. Teachers have families and loved ones too.

They finally gave up, hugs and kisses and tearful goodbyes with promises that they'd be back as soon as times got better. But they didn't get better and the schools were lost to vagabonds and homeless people. It only fed Madge's anger. She was angry at everyone back then. She was angry at the mayor, the governor and the president. She was angry at the school board and the city council. She organized a group of parents and marched on the streets but after a while there was no one left to protest and no one left to hear them.

She remembered when people always criticized the schools. Teachers were overpaid and got too much time off. But when hard times came, they hung on longer than the police, the firefighters, the prisons and the hospitals. Madge was angry at all of them.

Her anger finally played itself out when Charlie, her youngest, only five and still as innocent as the day she was born, apologized for dropping her spoon on the kitchen floor. Madge realized that she was just about to go off. She realized the damage she was doing to her daughter's young mind and to Denim, her older son, as well. It was not possible. It was not acceptable. It was not who she was.

She turned the anger and the blame against herself. She told herself she didn't understand when her husband needed her to understand. She didn't give me enough support when I was down. I was a man. I was supposed to be strong and she leaned on me when I needed someone to lean on. She turned herself inside out and finally she decided to look for me.

It was a sort of madness but it was something she had to do. She had always tried to do the right thing for the children. When the schools shut down she taught the kids herself. She worked hard on the garden and did more than her share of the cooking and cleaning but her mind was divided. A part of her was always thinking of me. She had to find me before she could move on.

At first she didn't know where to look. Every park in town was a camp of homeless people. Every public building, every abandoned storefront, every shopping mall was a shelter for the growing number who had lost their homes. Every foreclosed home for that matter was now just another roof for whoever claimed it. She went to see our old home and found it falling apart with overgrown weeds, broken windows and doors. It was trashed. She wondered why they even bothered to kick people out of their homes when the result was so obvious. There was no place for people to go.

She started looking in the parks. She made a copy of a photograph and handed it out. She stapled some to trees and telephone poles. She asked everyone she came across: Have you seen this man? If you do, tell him to come home. Tell him we love him and we need him.

The things she saw frightened her. Every park was barren. A few patches of grass, makeshift gardens, tents and cardboard shelters, mounds of garbage everywhere, people crowded together, men, women and children. The kids had no room to play, no place to bathe and not enough food or clean drinking water. Some of the trees were being chopped up for firewood. And the smell, the stench emanating from the restrooms. They must have stopped working months ago. People did what they had to do. They designated an area and buried their waste with a shovel. It was horrifying. They were destroying their own living space but what choice did they have? In the beginning, the police tried to keep order but they soon gave up. By then, there were so few police left they never bothered to come to the parks or the shelters unless there was a riot. And there were riots. That's what people do when they're hungry. That's what people do when the authorities let them down. That's what fathers do when they can't take care of their families. It's what mothers do when their children have no safe place in the world - no schools, no parks, no playgrounds. They explode in rage and they tear things down.

You learn not to see. You learn to filter it out. At least Madge had a purpose. She was looking for her children's father. That's all she could do. She taught the children at home every day: two or three hours of reading, writing and math. She made lunch and saw to it they ate. Then she went out to the parks. When she had covered the nearby parks, she got on a bike and went to the others. At first and for a time Denim went with her but she worried that it made him so sad when they came up empty. She was relieved when he decided not to go. His young tears and the downward expression of disappointment was more than she could handle. He wiped away the tears but the feeling would stay with him like a shadow on his life.

She rode all over town. She made a grid and covered it methodically. She rode by the stores she used to shop in, the restaurants where we used to eat, the novelty shops, art galleries, department stores, card shops, bakeries, fast food stops, office supplies, banks, clothing and jewelry stores – all of them closed, boarded up or looted. The malls were a disaster. She couldn't believe how fast it had happened. All of these places were once the center of someone's life. How could it all crumble so quickly?

She saw stacks of plastic containers, bags and broken down appliances on every street corner. Even so it wasn't as bad as one would think. After the early days when the stench of raw sewage overwhelmed, people learned. Everything that could be burned was either burned or stored for later. There was very little edible garbage or refuge. People ate what they had and what couldn't be eaten was used in gardens. Human waste was buried. People planted gardens everywhere there was good soil. It was a new way of life. People worked in them and protected them from harm. Water and containers were reused.

They say there's always good in bad times and I guess this is it. The scent of fresh fruit and vegetables on the vine traveled down the lanes and roads, breathing hope into the people that we would survive. As long as we can breathe we will find a way.

She met all kinds of people on her search. She tried to stand apart. The last thing she wanted was to get involved in other people's lives but she couldn't help caring. People who had come from high paying jobs working alongside people who had worked with their hands all their lives, pulling together, working together, taking care of each other's children. In so many ways it warmed her heart.

Finally, someone recognized the man in the picture. She was at a park at the north end of town and a man who was busy repairing fabric for tents took a look and looked again. Yes, he had seen that face and if memory served him it was at the Bridge Camp across the river at the south end of town. He couldn't be sure but he thought it was his face and he thought that was the place.

It's too late in the day to make it to the bridge before nightfall so she decides to go home. On the ride she thinks things through, sorting through mixed emotions. She understands why I did what I did but she also knows that many families managed to stay together. Why hadn't ours? There's joy in the possibility that she now knows where her husband might be but there are also misgivings. Months have passed since we were together. What if I'm with someone else? What if I don't want to come home? She can't be sure of anything, even that I will be there, so she decides not to tell the kids or anyone else at home. She will stick to her schedule. She will take care of the kids, work in the garden and then ride to the Bridge Camp to see if her long lost husband is there. She will ask if he wants to see his children. How can I say no? I can't. Not if I'm the same man she knows and loves. I will have no choice.

She doesn't sleep much that night. She knows she will dream of me and she doesn't want that. She wants her mind to be clear and open. She wants to look in my eyes and see if my love for her is still there. She wants to be sure of her love for me. She wants to listen without judgment. She wants no anger, no retribution and no blame. She goes over and over it in her mind. How she will look and what she will say. She tries not to bend the conversation to her will. She tries to see the world from my eyes and uses the thoughts and words that come from my heart.

Restless and tired when the morning finally arrives, she goes through the motions and gets through the day. She kisses Denim and Charlie before she leaves and they both give her that strange look that tells you they know something is up. She wants to tell them but she can't. She can't risk the disappointment. She won't.

Riding through the old neighborhood on her way to the bridge her surroundings turn a hazy gray. She stops to gain her bearings. An older man asks if she needs help and she almost panics. She thanks him and rides on. The more she thinks the less she understands. When she finally reaches the old bridge with its statuesque guardian lions, worn and cracked with age, the only thought she has left is that she wants her husband back. If necessary she will join me under the bridge. She will bring the children along. As long as we can be together we will make it work.

She walks over the bridge trailing her bike at her side, unsteady and trembling, her heart throbbing like a migraine. She can hardly see for the tears that she cannot stop from welling in her eyes. She sits down to breathe as soon as she clears the bridge. She sees some of the people from the camp below going about their business, gathering wood, collecting berries, tending the gardens and doing whatever it is they have to do to survive. They look like regular people, not the haggard homeless bunch they used to ignore as much as possible. They look just like anyone else in hard times. She imagines being one of them.

A woman notices her and smiles. She stops her gardening and walks up the dirt trail to where Madge still sits, unable to stir. Sitting beside her she asks her name. It puts Madge strangely at ease. It occurs to her how rare it is to have someone ask your name these days. "I'm Madge."

She introduces herself as Solar. She belongs to the generation of unusual names. They shake hands and share the view. It's a pleasant day, still warm though autumn is winding in, and they sit and talk about the weather and how good it is for the gardens and the people working to survive the coming winter. They talk about the change in their lives and how it isn't all bad. People are learning to live together. People are returning to the earth. While we still burn wood for heat, the poisoning of the air and water on an industrial scale has mostly stopped and the planet is slowly healing.

Finally Madge tells her why she's here and shows

her the picture. Solar doesn't hesitate. We're friends. She tells her that I was in camp when she arrived. She says I'm an honest man, hard working and giving. I had helped her set up camp when a spot opened. She was alone and a little lonely but I never tried to take advantage. She feels warm toward me and frankly wouldn't have minded if I had. But I did not.

Solar speaks quietly and with caution and hesitation before delivering the news that Madge has come for. I had left only yesterday morning. Solar got up early just to say goodbye and wish me well.

She asks Madge how we're related and Madge tells her we're married. She just nods. It's a story she has heard dozens of times. Many families have been torn apart. She was living with a man herself when hard times hit. They didn't last two weeks. He left without a word and she was out in the streets when the bills came in. It was back in the days when gas companies and rental agencies still expected you to pay. She found her way to the Bridge Camp and was lucky that someone had just departed. She had her place, she felt safe and she was comfortable but she was worried about surviving the winter outdoors. They were building a wall to block the western wind and they had plenty of wood for burning but she was still worried. They all worried. They know that some of them will not make it. They can only hope that most of them will.

"You should talk to Sugar," she says suddenly.

She tells her all about the man who took me under his wing. She explains that he's a kind of teacher. He teaches survival skills and helps people prepare for the road. If anyone knows where I'm headed, she says, it's Sugar.

She helps Madge down the hill, sits her at her

campsite and heats up some water over a wood-burning stove for tea while they wait for Sugar. He's working on a new greenhouse and shelter in the orchards up river. Madge worries that she won't make it home before nightfall but she feels she must talk to the man. She has to know where I went and what I was thinking. She can't go home without answers.

Sugar comes walking into camp with a couple others not long before sundown. They walk out to meet him and he seems to know who Madge is without asking. His expression slowly changes from joy to sorrow as he realizes why she has come.

"You missed him by a day and a half," he says.

His gaze is downward, as if studying the ground beneath his feet, his remorse so sincere that for a moment Madge thinks he's to blame. But anyone with half the sense of a blue jay can see his remorse rides on sympathy, not guilt. Madge recognizes right away this man is like her husband, a decent man doing the best he can to ease the burden on his fellow travelers. He has the kind of face that reveals the hardship of years of struggle. Life has not been kind to Sugar but nothing he has encountered so far can defeat his gentle and giving spirit.

They sit in his campsite in the cool of the evening, a soft wind singing through the trees, more thoughts than they can manage to speak. Sugar tells her what I told him, my reasons for leaving, reflecting my love and good will. Madge relates her side of the story.

Solar listens to both of them, remaining silent, letting the words flow on a warm current of empathy. Sugar's story ends with me departing camp on my way south with instructions to take the untraveled roads. He tells her I have a vague idea of going to see my family in Colorado but he considers it unlikely I will make that journey.

"Most likely he ends up in some other camp down the road. He'll find shelter for the winter and then he'll come back home in the spring."

Madge allows that thought to settle as the camp comes to life with people preparing for the evening meal. She thinks about following my path south on the hope that she can still find me if fate is on her side. Sugar advises against it. It's a hard road even for a well-traveled man. It's far too dangerous for a woman alone. Solar nods in agreement, as if the road has been cruel to her as well, and reminds Madge of her kids.

Of course, she thinks. Fate has already made its play. She will go home to be with her children and her husband will travel on alone. It's not what she wants and not what she imagined but she still has hope that my road will wind back home. She will wait for the spring.

The sun falling from the sky, a mellow sunset just blooming over the trees and blanketing the foliage to the west of the camp, it's far too late to ride back home. Sugar asks her to stay the night. She knows he's right. Her family will be worried but they would be fine. The worry would end at daylight. Solar and Sugar see to it that she's fed and fixed up with a place to sleep, a couple of wool blankets and a makeshift pillow.

They have a camp bonfire with music and singing, dancing and good times. Sugar pulls a few home brewed beers out of his stash and shares them.

Madge is surprised at how good she feels. She feels warmth. She feels wanted. For one night there are no expectations, no struggles with the family, no arguments or pressures. For one night she lets all the emotions she keeps contained inside float out into the last of a summer breeze. She and Sugar and Solar talk into the late night – mostly about the future they envision, the ones they can paint with the brushes of desire – and then she sleeps. She sleeps more soundly and deeply than she has in months.

In the morning she thanks them and promises she'll come back to the camp whenever she can and she'll bring her children to meet them. They smile as if she's only being polite but she means it very sincerely. She wants them to be a part of their lives. She wants the children to see how other people live. If their father never comes back, she wants them to be a bridge to his memory. Children need to remember the good.

She rides back to her mother's house and calls Denim and Charlie into their room. She tells them a story about their father. It's a different story than the one they know. It's a story of a man doing his best under the most difficult circumstances, a man who loves his wife and children enough to take on the hardships of the road. She tells them he will return as soon as he can. She says that spring is the best they can hope for.

They seemed pleased with her story. Denim has that look of knowing that children develop at a certain age. He's glad his mother has come to terms with his father's absence but he doesn't really believe I will ever come back. He knows too many others whose parents have split apart and never came back together. But Charlie believes. Her eyes shine with delight even through her tears when her mother says they will have to wait for spring. Madge wipes her tears away, kisses her on both cheeks, and prays she will not have to tell another story come spring.

Everyone in the family notices the change that comes over Madge when she returns. When she finally learned what had become of me, that I had lived under that bridge until I left town, it was as though her lungs filled with fresh air. She's convinced I'm all right and that I will return home eventually. At least that's what she chooses to believe and what she chooses to project to her family. She's aware of making that choice. It enables her to move on with her life in a manner that benefits everyone.

Her mother is not so certain. Grace has seen too much of the world to believe in happy endings. It's a cold harsh world out there. In hard times, there's nothing you can be sure of. But she keeps her doubts to herself and welcomes the change in her daughter's heart. As only the wise and the old know, there is always a blessing in misfortune – especially if one is lucky enough to survive it.

They settle back into their daily routine as best they can. Madge resolves to be a peacemaker in the home as much as possible. She tries hard to understand everyone's point of view. She compliments Joan every chance she has though it's not easy to find suitable opportunities. She works extra hard to win over Joan's kids. They're sweet kids really. All kids are sweet. They just want to be loved and to know the rules. She works on her relationship with Carlin and encourages Uncle Bud and Aunt Mildred to engage in family discussions.

Madge soon becomes the center of the home. She helps shape them into a caring, loving family despite their differences. She becomes a social activist, organizing the neighbors, making sure all the children are cared for, handing out books and inviting children from the neighborhood to school in their living room.

They all make an effort to give Grace the respect she deserves. It's her house and it's not her fault the whole world turned upside down. If she wants something, someone would get it for her. If she makes a decision, it's up to the family to carry it out. Eventually, she will emerge from her self-imposed isolation and become the strong and loving woman the family had known before the fall.

Madge's thinking changes on education. Of course reading, writing and math are important, very important, but there are new skills the children need just as much. They study gardening and alternative energy systems. They study nutrition and water conservation. She goes to the library every Thursday (the library is still functioning with volunteers who believe that books are the most important legacy we can preserve for future generations) and brings home a selection of books for reading: Science books on greenhouse effects and climatology, books on the sun and the stars, history books on the Great Depression, industrialization, immigrant movements, the pilgrims, slavery, women's rights, civil rights, the Civil War, the World Wars, the Cold Wars, the displacement of indigenous tribes and westward migration. She wants her children to know that every generation has challenges and if they work hard and keep their eyes looking forward they too will overcome.

She brings home great books of literature: *The Grapes of Wrath, Blood Meridian, A Day in the Life of Ivan Denisovich, The Lord of the Rings, Adventures of Huckleberry Finn, Don Quixote, Moby Dick, The Wizard of Oz, The Last of the Mohicans, Invisible Man, Frankenstein, The Three Musketeers, Robinson Crusoe, 1984, A Brave New*

*World*. She no longer cares about reading level. She wants the children to appreciate the sound of words and the wonderful stories they tell. They take turns reading aloud just for the sound and rhythm and then they retell the stories in their own words.

Madge is never sure if it's her efforts that make a difference in the home. She's sure that if anyone asks Joan she'll swear it's something *she* did. Whatever it is things get better around the house. The adults are more respectful of each other and the children become friends. Maybe it's inevitable. When people realize there is no viable option, they begin to adjust. No one volunteers to live in hell.

In November they receive word that a nasty virus is hitting communities in the northern part of the valley. It's headed their way. Whole communities and camps are laid out. A lot of people have died. The medicines they have (even if they were available) can only ease the suffering. Antibiotics no longer work. (They hadn't really worked for a long time.) No one knows where it came from or why but everyone seems afraid it's a modern version of the great plague. The religious freaks are out in mass with their signs forecasting the end of the world as if the ultimate prize is noticing.

The family gets together with their neighbors and decides to put up barriers at both ends of their street to keep the vagabonds out. Some of the neighbors want to keep everyone out, friends and family included. Thank God they're voted down. Madge is not the only one who's waiting for a wandering family member to return. They all agree that if someone gets sick they will quarantine the house. Before it's over two houses will be quarantined and three people will die, two of them children. That's the great shame of epidemic illnesses. It takes the young and innocent along with the old and weak first. It's the way of the world and though it's hard on all, it makes the survivors tougher, stronger and more determined than ever.

They knew those children. They were a little younger than Charlie but she played with them often enough. Madge can't tell you how many times Charlie asked why she can't go to the Parker house any more. She doesn't understand that some sicknesses are deadly. She can't wrap her mind around disease and death. Even after they've been gone for weeks and months, she still asks about them and wonders when they will return. Like her father.

What do you tell a child who has no concept of death? Madge tells her the truth. They're dead and buried. They're not coming back. She's afraid Charlie still doesn't understand but she appreciates her mother trying to explain. She welcomes the comfort of her voice and the warmth of her embrace. Only when Madge cries does she. Even that carries a strange and relieving comfort.

Denim gets it. He knows people are dying all the time. He sees them on his bicycle rides. Madge fears he's becoming too hard, too immune to the emotions that a child his age should have. She supposes everyone grows up faster in hard times. We work hard. We have little time for grief or mourning. We move on. It's our job to keep on moving. It's the only way forward and the best way to survive.

When the winds bring the first chill of winter the family is prepared. They have a good supply of fruits and vegetables they've canned themselves. The greenhouse is up and running. They have a solar panel that Carlin salvaged from an abandoned house, a generator and a small supply of gas. They have a wood stove and plenty of wood cut to size.

Come December, two weeks short of Christmas, they're beginning to feel assured. They're beginning to have confidence that they can make it through the winter and if they can make it through the first winter, why not the second and the third?

That's when the tornadoes hit. There's no television or radio so they have no other warning than what they can see with their own eyes and hear with their own ears. There's a beautiful strangeness in the sky. It's stunning. The clouds, especially near sundown, paint a picture of another world, with swirling, twisting, bold and magnificent colors.

The weather turns unseasonably warm for this time of year and anyone who has ever lived in Oklahoma or Missouri can tell you it looks like tornado weather.

# DAY OF THE TWISTERS

It's late afternoon and Madge is out in the garden, weeding, hoeing, checking the drip system and picking a few of the remaining tomatoes for supper when the temperature drops and a shadow draws over her. She hears the wind but she doesn't feel it. She hears what sounds like pebbles dropping on the plastic covering of their greenhouse and roof. She looks up and the clouds are writhing in spectacular formations with flashes of turquoise and streaks of purple, orange and black. She gets up and walks out into the yard where she can get a clear view and sees two, then three funnel clouds streaking in their direction.

The wind begins to sing as she rushes inside to tell everyone to take cover. They don't have a basement or a storm shelter. This is California where things like this never happen. Well, they never used to happen. In recent years, even before the crash, extreme weather has become more and more common. Our leaders know why it's happening but they either don't believe we can do anything about it or they don't care.

They all crowd into the bathroom where Carlin drags two mattresses from the beds and the adults pull them over for protection as the windows shake and the storm's rage screams so loud they have to cover their ears. The children cry like banshees and Grace is breathing so hard Madge thinks she's having a heart attack.

It passes in no more than thirty seconds but it feels like the end of the world. They wait another five minutes, clutching to each other, just in case they're in the eye of the storm.

Grace is transported back to when she was a little girl. It must have been October because she was standing in the pumpkin patch playing drums on the pumpkins when her mother yells at her to come in. She thinks she's in trouble for wearing her Sunday dress outside. She looks up and freezes. It's the most beautiful sight she has ever seen: a magnificent sky full of colors and wild shapes formed of clouds. Her father sweeps her up in his arms and takes her down to the cellar where they all hunch together, holding their breaths and feeling the drumbeat of their hearts. The whole house shakes and it sounds like they're standing underneath a large jet as it takes off.

Only then she didn't know that sound. It sounds like the end of the world. Somehow it steals the oxygen right out of the air and leaves you gasping. The pumpkin patch was a mess but the family was unharmed. The storm passed and they survived.

Carlin is strong in a pinch and Madge is a rock. The two of them take charge and make sure everyone is safe. It's horrifying but they survive. They feel stronger because they survive. They are survivors and they can handle whatever God has in mind though some might have questioned for a time God's relentless vindictiveness. What more will they have to endure? When will it be enough to appease God's need for suffering? Does it even matter that the innocent suffer along with the guilty?

Grace had given up organized religion a long time ago but she remains a spiritual person. She prays on the day of the twisters. In the event that there is a God and that he or she or it whatever it is can hear their prayers, she prays.

Denim is so scared he almost drops his tough guy demeanor until he looks at his sister. Charlie is shaking so hard he thinks the tornado has somehow got inside her. She shakes for hours after the twisters are long gone. Madge and Grace take turns holding her and Denim stays by her side, taking her hand and stroking her shoulder. *It's all right. Nothing can hurt us now. It's okay.* He's with her when she finally takes a breath and remembers where she is, when she remembers the love that surrounds her and protects her from harm.

Some would say it was a series of nine twisters, one after another, some weaker, some stronger, but they tear whole neighborhoods and camps apart. Buildings twisted like children's toys, homes and trees uprooted, cars, vans and trucks tossed onto roofs. It sounded like locusts, a sea of humming beasts, a roar of pounding waves; it was so loud and so relentless. When it got close it rumbled the earth.

They're lucky. Their house is untouched. The gods of tornados are gods of chance like a roulette wheel. They spin their horrors, twisting and winding and cracking like a whip and when they pass and the shock of the pounding volume subsides and the pressure that steals all sense of balance eases, they're left to witness who the monster claims. In their neighborhood it claims a house on the corner and one across the street. It could just as easily have been them. They're lucky or blessed or marked for another trial – whatever one's beliefs allow.

The people in the fallen houses are lucky too. They still have their lives. They're badly bruised and scraped up but the monster has no appetite for human flesh. Not this time. It wants only brick and mortar in their corner of town.

The neighbors take them in – the ones that still have a little spare room – and they all agree to contribute food, wood, whatever it takes to make up for what they lost. Their confidence is shaken. The whole town was hit. They have no way of knowing how much damage is done. They have no way of knowing whether anyone in the government can help or if they care or if they even know what's happening. They know better than to expect help from anyone.

In the tick of a clock their supplies suddenly do not look so plentiful. They go back to work: expanding their greenhouses, collecting and cutting wood, making repairs and improvements. The twisters have shaken their confidence but it does not weaken their resolve. If anything they are more determined than before. They are conditioned by now to expect adversity. They will never back down. Or so they believe.

At a time when no one else can do so, Madge sees to it that Christmas is something they will always cherish. They have all been so serious for so long it's as if they forgot how to laugh and sing and play. She gets every neighbor on the street involved, from the oldest to the youngest. Everyone is given a responsibility. She even talks the stodgy Bannisters (owners of the largest house on the block) into hosting the event in their spacious back yard.

It's a glorious event. They have music and dance and games and every face wears a smile that lasts the entire evening. There are gifts for every child and old man Bannister plays the unlikely part of Santa. Scrooge would have been more fitting. The sound of laughter is the sweetest music of all.

They have home grown wine and the finest array of garden vegetables and fruit pies ever assembled. They have catfish and nuts and cashews and chocolates from the Caribbean and coffee, sweet delicious coffee from somewhere down south. They have cookies and cakes, olives and grapes, and bakery delights with sliced almonds and rare spices.

There's no turkey and no ham. Since food became scarce people stopped raising animals for meat. It's more efficient and economical to raise crops for direct consumption. People still eat meat when they can but it comes from hunting, fishing and trapping rather than poultry farms or pig farms or cattle ranches. A little venison, catfish and rabbit stew is enough to make the occasion special.

The children all have gifts from Santa. There's licorice and cotton candy and jelly babies and fudge and strawberries and blueberry jams and dolls carved of wood and models of castles and log cabins. There are books: whatever book a child desires is hers or his forever. There are toys that move as if by magic and toys that spark imagination.

It's a beautiful Christmas. It's the most beautiful Christmas in the history of the world. They have peace. They have their basic needs fulfilled. They have a good idea of what tomorrow will bring and they are ready to face the challenge. It's a Christmas of hope. With so much loss and so much suffering they enjoy a rebirth of spirit that spreads joy and gratitude.

Elsewhere it is the same. Madge brings the children to the Bridge Camp on Christmas Eve. They bring gifts of fine foods, trinkets and toys, wine and spirits. They bring the thanks and blessings of their family and friends. They bring the spirit of love and unity and they receive more than they give.

Madge will never forget this Christmas as long or as short as she lives. It will be one of her last memories. She sees her youngest child Charlie bloom as a human being. She finds her rhythm, her step and her calling. She becomes a dancer, a singer and a person with opinions. Her son Denim, who has matured before he should have, discovers the joy of life that is Christmas for the first time and it will never abandon him again.

They are content and filled with hope. The hardships they have overcome together make them closer. The family is secure and they are a part of a community. They have confidence that their neighbors will help them just as they will help their neighbors.

After Christmas they settle in, mending the clothes, tending the greenhouse, making household repairs, canning and stocking and finding new ways to spend the night. Without television, radio or the Internet they learn how to carry on conversations. They find board games stored away in the garage – monopoly, checkers, chess, trivia – and they play for hours before they retire for the evening. It's like those old pioneer movies and television series that no one quite remembers.

It's quiet. It's so quiet you can hear a dog barking blocks away. You can hear a neighbor's argument or someone walking on the street with hard-heeled shoes. No one can move around outside at night without drawing all eyes and ears. It's strangely reassuring.

The winter is so mild they hardly ever have to light a fire. They wear layers of clothing and wool sweaters and drape a blanket over their laps. The kids huddle with their parents and grandparents, exchanging the warmth of their bodies. There in the arms of loving adults the children are secure in the belief, grounded more on faith than on anything more tangible, that nothing can bring them harm.

# THE SHAKEDOWN

They are almost comfortable and nearly content when the visitors arrive. Visitors. That's a euphemism for what they actually are. Looking back it was probably inevitable. There are those who prepare for the winter and those who do not. When the food runs out they come looking. Some say they're gangsters from the big cities who migrated to the valley where fewer people compete for greater resources. We would later hear it's the last phase of a mass prisoner release, hardened criminals, violent and unprepared to survive in the world by any other means.

It's not difficult to put the pieces together. They closed down the prisons and jails. What point is there in having a jail when half the population would volunteer as prisoners? Free meals and a roof over your head outweighs the bars that prevent escape. So hardened criminals are released into the world where there's no place for them to survive. When the food runs short and they have no shelter, they take what they need in the only way they know how.

Whoever they are and whatever their reasons the neighborhood is not prepared for what they offer. The three of them show up late one evening when everyone is inside. They bang a couple of garbage can lids together until the residents come out. They're not tall but broad, wearing leather jackets and carrying clubs, chains and knives. Once the people are assembled, the men and a handful of women with baseball bats and garden tools, the thugs inform them there's trouble coming, big trouble, and they offer protection. They say they have an army that can fight back any enemy. In exchange, they want a supply of food.

The neighbors listen to what they have to say and everyone understands: These thugs want to feed themselves with the community produce, fruits and vegetables they had grown with their own hands, canned and stored, and in exchange they will protect the neighborhood from themselves. It's a common shakedown and once it begins it has no end. They will take a little at first, and then a little more and more, until no family has enough to eat.

They look at each other in fear and skepticism and a man who considers himself a community leader speaks for them all: *We need time to talk it over.* The three thugs smile and rattle their chains, playfully tapping their clubs in their hands, and one of them says they will be back in two or three days to hear the community's decision.

"Talk all you want!" he says. "These boys are coming and they're not like us. They'll take everything you got and they won't ask you nice!"

Thankfully none of the men act on their impulse to challenge them then and there. Big John and Jose bite their lips and hold back. They feel like their manhood is being challenged. It is. But more than anything else they need time to think and make plans no matter what they ultimately decide to do. There are the children and the old folks to think about.

They call a neighborhood meeting first thing after dinner. Gathering at the Bannister's every house is represented. Everyone agrees it's a shakedown and the visitors can't be trusted. There's no guarantee they will keep their word. In fact no one believes they will. Still, there's no agreement on what they should do. Most of the men led by Big John and Jose want to fight. Several of them have fancy hunting bows and arrows. They want to collect weapons and set up defenses. The women are divided. Some think they have no choice. They have to fight. If they give in God knows what will happen: rape, kidnapping, child abuse, it all comes into play. Others think they should at least try negotiating. It will give them more time to prepare. Maybe the authorities will come to their aid. Maybe they can get the children and the elderly out of harm's way.

They decide to send a runner to the only remaining police center. Who would have thought that a city of this size would be down to one police station?

In the beginning, when things went bad but the police and firefighters and public health officials still had paying jobs, and the police were still holding on to their authority, they thought it was their responsibility to protect the rich. But the rich never reciprocated, never shared the wealth, and never even thought about the families of the people protecting them. When that reality took hold everything changed.

When the money ran out volunteers took over nearly all public services. They receive extra food and gas coupons and that's fine because money has lost most of its value. Some people hoard money in anticipation of a return to normalcy but even that expectation is fading. There would have been thousands of volunteers but there's a strict limit. There isn't enough food and gas is a luxury. The police that remain are obviously overstretched. They are ex-police officers, security people and military personnel. The neighborhood has asked for their help before – to deal with thieves mostly – and they never come. They don't expect help this time either but they feel they have to try. If they don't come for this they can be sure they will never come so they won't even bother to ask again.

Having made no decision and not knowing what would happen with the police, they have no choice but to start working on their defenses. Having been in the military Carlin gets involved in the planning, training and preparations. Some of the neighbors still have guns and ammunition stashed away but not enough to make a difference. It's the only crime that still matters, using a firearm. They'll use them if they have to but only as a last resort. Only if their lives depend on it. If they use them they'll face the consequences. The authorities will take everything they have and tear the neighborhood apart looking for more.

They have half a dozen high tech bows, three of them the smaller hand-held variety and three more traditional bows. Each has a dozen arrows. They set up targets and start practicing in the back yard of the Bannister house. They plan to place them on roofs at each end of the street, looking down on the barricades.

They gather a dozen or so baseball bats, wood and metal, and distribute them to able-bodied men and women. They have chains, golf clubs, stones and baseballs, clubs fashioned from the handles of brooms and garden tools. They have axes, hatchets and butcher knives. They strengthen their barricades with old stoves and refrigerators, cars and trucks, anything they can find.

They are all agreed there's no choice but to fight but they know they're not the kind of people who can fight effectively against criminals. There are too many old people like Grace and too many children like Denim and Charlie.

Madge looks around at the assortment of weapons and the people that are supposed to use them and all she can think is what a disaster it will be if they really have to fight. She waits until the day is over and dinner's on the table to ask Carlin what he thinks. He's tired and agitated and the sweat from his hard work and worry make his skin shine in the candlelight. He shakes his head and his face turns dark. He doesn't want to say it's hopeless. In his mind there's no choice. If these people have a large force and they're allowed inside the gates, he's certain they will take everything. Everyone in the neighborhood will either be forced out of their own homes or worse. He believes they will move some of the people out and use the rest as they please: slaves for cooking, cleaning, farm labor, sex and sport.

He knows the community is not ready to face them down. Maybe they will never be ready. They are not fighters but they are survivors. His one hope is that the neighborhood can put up enough of a fight that their enemy will choose to move on. There are many other neighborhoods that have as much and more than they have and some of them will open the doors of negotiations. If they put up a resistance, if they make the gangsters pay a price, if they show they're willing to fight, that might be enough.

He feels strongly that the women, children and the elderly should be evacuated even though he has no clue where – anywhere but here is his only thought. Madge says they should think of their own family first and they should start thinking now while there's still time.

All the adults are at the table while the kids play in the living room. Everyone is quiet, waiting to hear what Carlin says next. All the weight of the family falls on his shoulders and Madge wishes I were there to lighten the load. Carlin was not born to be a leader. He fills the void because it's his responsibility as a man. He feels things deeply but he's learned to hold his feelings in. He's become stoic over the years and others count on him to remain cool and collected. He's feeling the pressure now and it registers on his face. He's anguished and slow to speak. When he does they are all the more ready to listen.

He says that if their family is having this discussion they can be sure that others are as well. He says they have to think beyond tomorrow. Even if they can find a place where they would be safe for a day or a week, they would still have to survive the winter. Even if they survive the winter they would have to start over with nothing. He reflects that things look grim but at least they have a plan. If they stick together they have a chance. If they fall apart they have no chance.

Everyone nods in agreement and even Madge has to surrender. There are no viable options. Carlin informs them that he'll find a temporary safe haven in the morning. He assures everyone that he can find a place within the area. They will offer food for shelter and someone will take them in. Then they will transport the children, the old people and the mothers. He says that he has broached the subject with Big John but there isn't enough time to come to a decision. He's sure everyone will agree.

Madge feels better knowing they will at least try to get the children out but she also knows there are a lot of problems and she can see many of them. The roads aren't safe with these criminals roaming around. How can they transport children and old people? If the criminal gangs hit their neighborhood, why wouldn't they have hit others in the area? How far will they have to go? How much food will they have to promise? Why would others believe them, trust them, risk their own welfare for someone else?

If they lose the neighborhood, there will be no food. Some of the old people can't walk. Some are sick. Some of the children are only infants or toddlers. There are so many problems and so little time. Madge goes over all the scenarios she can think of and all of them end in disaster.

The surest way to work up a crusade...is to promise people they will have a chance of maltreating someone. To be able to destroy with good conscience...is the height of psychological luxury.

Aldous Huxley
*Crome Yellow*

# THE RESCUE

Late at night they receive good news. Their runner returns with word that the military is on its way. The police center has a short wave radio connection to the military base. They were already tracing the movement of the Folsom gang (named for the prison that had been their home). The gang started out as common thieves and thugs, taking what they needed and moving on. As they made their way south they got bolder and more violent. By the time they hit their part of the central valley they lost all sense of decency and restraint. They were taking over whole neighborhoods and small towns. There is no longer any doubt what they intend to do here.

They leave a trail of blood and horror wherever communities decide to fight back. They're not afraid to lose some of their own so long as they prevail. It's a price they're willing to pay. The more a community resists the greater the pain they inflict. Carlin is right: rape, enslavement and torture are to be expected. The gang holds public executions by hanging and beheading. In one case they reportedly quartered a man.

Worse news still, they picked up recruits as they go

along. What began as a predominantly Latino gang is now multi-ethnic and diverse, its members virtually unidentifiable. They are becoming a threat to the established order or what remains of it and that is why they've become a target to the police and government forces.

The military does not have the resources to fight this threat everywhere they go so they decide to make a stand in this suburban neighborhood. They roll in three transport vehicles in the early morning hours and evacuate everyone but a handful of men. Carlin is one of those who stay behind. A few of the local men are needed to carry out the plan. Big John, Jose, Carlin and a couple of others will greet the gangsters at the barricade to inform them that the neighborhood has decided to refuse their offer. Then they will wait for the gang to assemble in full force.

The rest of the neighbors are taken to a large warehouse with a concrete floor, metal walls and a high metal roof. There are barriers to shield the civilians from the soldiers as they conduct their training exercises. It's cold – not so much physically as emotionally. There's no human touch. The soldiers do what they can to make them comfortable: laying down rugs, bringing out toys, books, small chairs and tables for the children and board games for both kids and adults. They serve warm meals twice a day and an officer gives them regular updates on the developments at home. It's always a little vague and stiff as if he has rehearsed and performed these duties a dozen times before.

An officer tells them there's little chance of anything going wrong. They not only have powerful weapons and an unlimited supply of ammunition, they are the elite soldiers of former wars. The Folsom gang is no match for them. He never says it will be a massacre. He doesn't need to say it. These are criminals who crossed the line and there are no prisons or jails to put them in. Justice and mercy are the first casualties of the new order. People know – they had to know – but they put it aside. Survival is all that matters.

The families of the old neighborhood feel trapped inside their quarters. The commander won't allow them to go outside – as if they would give away the location, as if anyone would choose to attack their fortress. They set up an indoor walkway, barricaded so they can't see what's going on, so they can't tell anyone about the weapons they have. It's strange and cold.

They're saddened and disappointed. People aren't meant to live as captives. It warps the senses. Children are meant to run and play in the sun and breathe the open air. Try as they may, neither Madge nor Grace nor any of the other parents can understand that decision. What are they hiding? What are they afraid they will see? They can think of no rational reason for it but there's no means of challenging the commander's authority. When they talk to their information officer – a misnomer if ever there was one – he simply informs them it's camp regulations. They're going stir crazy. The children are restless and the adults are short-tempered.

One day some of the older kids manage to sneak outside and Denim is among them. He has a quiet but defiant spirit that Madge and I have always admired. Some of the soldiers catch them and haul them back inside. The kids are scared half to death. The soldiers tell them they will be locked up in a cage if it happens again. They order the families to discipline them and of course they agree but the punishment amounts to nothing. They're not allowed to participate in the games that evening but they don't seem to mind. They huddle together and talk in hushed tones about their great adventure.

Later that night Madge asks Denim what he saw. He tells her they snuck into a warehouse filled with rifles and ammunition, stacks and stacks of them from the floor to the ceiling. This was after all a nation of guns before the fall. All those guns and the all-important ammunition had to go somewhere. They understand then why the kids can't run around unsupervised but it is unrealistic to expect children not to be children.

Grace spends a lot of time reading and thinking about her late husband. She thinks he would have enjoyed this new world. In many ways he was suited to it. He resented that kids today have all the modern comforts, computers and video games and portable music players with thousands and thousands of songs, and cell phones that mean you're never really alone with your thoughts. He thought we were losing touch with the things that matter most: family and friends, picnics and camping in the great outdoors, trips to Yosemite and the Grand Canyon, the wonders and mysteries of nature. He lamented that we were losing our sense of the earth beneath our feet, the soil that gives us life. He would have loved building greenhouses and gardening. He would have loved evenings without television and young people without devices attached to their ears and engaging their minds every waking hour. Of course he would not have appreciated being confined to a military warehouse but that would end soon enough. Or would it?

141

Grace sympathizes with his point of view but she realizes – and she feels sure he did too deep within – that it's the natural cycle of life. Every generation of old folks laments the lost ways of days gone by. Every generation wants to stop the clock and move backwards in time. Until this generation it was only a futile and wistful dream but here they are. She believes Bill would have liked to witness it. He would have thrived in this harsh environment and he had the kind of knowledge that would have been valued. He had a sound understanding of electronics, mechanics and gadgetry. He could fix most anything from a transistor radio to an old truck as long as it didn't involve modern technology.

Grace's mind is losing some of its agility and she's beginning to become aware of it. She wonders when it started. Maybe it happened years ago when Bill passed away but no one noticed because she was alone, free to think as she pleased and do what she wanted. Now no one seems to notice because she's old and that's how old people are. There are no more health centers, hospitals or doctors to tend to old people losing their faculties. They are what they are. There are no more drugs to fight back time or stop the aging process from taking its toll. Old people once again die from natural causes rather than dying in hospitals from infections or unpronounceable diseases when the insurance money runs out. She sometimes wonders if she has become cynical or has merely suppressed it until it no longer matters. Life is full of mysteries to occupy the mind.

She spends whole days on a single track of thought, so much so that she hardly notices the days passing. Being enclosed in the cavernous space of a military warehouse makes her condition such as it is worse. She spends so much of her time in memories that when she awakens each morning she often expects that Bill will be lying beside her. She speaks to anyone about the first time they met. She was the counter waitress at a diner and he was the first customer of the day. He was looking for work and needed a sympathetic listener. That first day he asked her if she wanted children. She said she did between cups of coffee. It was six months before he asked her out and a year before they got married. He was working then as a mechanic at a local garage and even then he was saving to start his own air conditioning business. It was the future he said.

She remembers their first child's second birthday. Uncle Bud dresses up in a clown costume and little Billy laughs until he's dizzy. They are so happy. They have nothing or next to nothing – a small furnished apartment at $65 dollars a month – but they're happy. Their hearts break when Billy dies. No one could explain it. One day he's playing and laughing and the next day he's gone. In many ways you never get over it but you learn to persevere.

Madge sees what's happening to her mother but she has her hands full with everything else that's going on. She speaks to her as often as she can and tries to keep her involved but time is one thing she doesn't have enough of. Grace is right. In this new world there's no time for the elderly. There's no time for the patience and special understanding the elderly require. It breaks Madge's heart when she allows herself to reflect on it but she has the children to think about. The children come first and no one understands that better than her mother.

It's something we would all have to think about: What do we do with the old folks? How do we use their knowledge, their wisdom, and incorporate them into the new social fabric? How can we make them feel wanted and loved? But we can't think about that as long as our very survival is at stake. We keep our noses to the pavement and march forward.

Madge does everything she can think of to establish a routine for the children. There's school every morning, walks around the enclosed walkway three times a day, and a variety of games. She spends virtually all her time with the children, reading and playing games and teaching them the wonders of a life they might never know again. She tells them about the Grand Canyon and the ocean and zoos and the Yosemite waterfalls. She tells them about running in the parks when the parks were still clean and green and full of squirrels and dogs chasing balls and jumping with joy. She sees the wonder in their young eyes and realizes how wondrous life really was before hard times. She wishes above all that I will return to share her thoughts and emotions.

On the third day their information officer informs them the Folsom gang scouts have come back to the neighborhood where they were told their offer has been refused. The officer says it's only a matter of time. They will be back and soon it will all be over. Three days later it is. They're told that their loved ones are safe and the Folsom gang will never bother us again. That's it. He doesn't take questions. He simply tells them they will leave in the morning.

They pack what little they have, climb in the transport vehicles and head back home. For some reason Madge pays attention to the direction they're going and the amount of time it takes. They travel east, where they take some turns and make some stops that she surmises are designed to disorient them, and then they go east again and then south. She figures out why they want to keep their location secret. They're not afraid of an assault. They aren't afraid of anything. But they don't want anyone to know their response time. It would take them a good 90 minutes to reach their town and another thirty to an hour to get to their neighborhood. An outlaw gang would have a good two hours to take and do whatever they want before the army can get there. Add a day or two for the information to travel and an outlaw gang would pretty much have free reign as long as they kept moving. No wonder the military wanted a showdown. It's the only way they can stop them.

As they near their destination, the transports stop and an information officer informs them there is some collateral damage. Collateral damage: That's the phrase the military uses whenever a large number of civilians are killed at war. Collateral damage has names like My Lai, Fallujah, Abu Ghraib, Hiroshima and Nagasaki. The use of that phrase is calculated to brace them for bad news. Some of their homes had been hit by firebombs. It was a contingency the soldiers were not prepared to counter or if they were they didn't think it was worth the effort. The information officer informs the civilians in their charge that some of them will have the option of returning to base until other living arrangements can be made.

Madge knows in her gut that their house is one of the damaged. She guesses others feel the same way and some of them are right. Three homes are burned beyond repair and their house is one of them. She doesn't know what to feel or rather she doesn't know how to handle the anger that she feels building within her. Should she be grateful that Carlin, the family and the neighbors are unharmed? Is it enough that the family is still together? She knows in her heart that the damage would have been much greater had the military not intervened but she resents that such choices were necessary. She has to wonder what kind of world they were creating for Charlie and Denim.

Carlin tells them later that he had to be restrained when the gang started its assault. The military wanted more numbers in the center of the street where they could mow them down with automatic weapons from the rooftops. They wiped them out. They killed them all and took the bodies away before the civilians arrived. They washed down the streets. Dozens, maybe a hundred people were killed and Madge for one couldn't help feeling sorry for them. The crimes they were held accountable for they hadn't had a chance to commit. Maybe they had in some other community but not here. Not in this place. How did she or anyone else know what they had done besides upsetting the natural order?

It seems that Carlin will never be the same. His stoicism before was a way to hide his feelings. Now it's deeper. It's real. There is something missing in his eyes. He's always somewhere else. He tells the family what he'd seen down to the gory details, the shock in their eyes, blood flooding the streets, the screams and the horror. He says with his eyes down as if hiding some unspeakable truth that no one could witness such a massacre and not be moved. It changes a man, even a man like him.

He remembers how it was before. He was not the kind to question authority. If the army said civilian casualties were unfortunate but unavoidable he believed them. When they said war was hell he agreed with them. He was in the first Gulf War. People said it wasn't much of a war and compared to the second maybe it wasn't but it was enough to give him a taste of what war is like. It was enough to give him the pride of a soldier like a player on a football team. Our side is always right. Of course they didn't take Baghdad. They never occupied the country. There was no Fallujah, Ramadi or Abu Ghraib. The people didn't hate them in that war even when they left Saddam Hussein in power and he wiped out the Kurds. That's all dead history now and nobody cares.

Carlin's a proud American and a patriot. Not the rah-rah type but people know where he stands. He speaks up when he feels he has to and he won't take crap from the crowd that always puts America down – like me and Madge for example. At least that's what Carlin thought. Before the crash we cared about things like that. Now? Now he doesn't know what he is: A homeless person, a hanger on, a taker and a leach. He has become the kind of person he had always blamed for what was wrong with this country.

He never really knew war in Iraq. He had to come back home for that. The soldiers drew them in and wiped them out. Caught them in a crossfire and laid them down. They used him and Big John to set the trap. They showed their faces, told them to go away and retreated to watch what followed. Carlin tried to stop them when they started throwing firebombs but they held him back and muzzled him. They didn't let him go until the fireworks began. Nice euphemism. They shot them down with automatic weapons. Snipers from the rooftops shot anyone who was still moving. Then they went man-to-man, body-to-body, in an operation they called Mercy Killing. Carlin watched every last kill. He had to watch. He didn't know why. He guessed some part of him figured the story needed to be told. Carlin was there so it fell to him. He was the one still standing. He was the one who absorbed it and lived. It was his story to tell.

The street was a river of blood and that was not a metaphor: a river of blood. If anyone survived they weren't in the street and they would never return. They'd get as far away as they could as fast as they could go and that was the point.

Carlin doesn't like talking about it but his mind keeps drifting back to that river of blood. The soldiers knew what they were doing. They brought high-powered hoses to wash the blood away. They wrapped the bodies in black plastic bags, stacked them up like heaps of garbage and hauled them away.

He shakes his head, looking as if he would almost cry, as if it was too much of a burden to carry. Now he doesn't speak of it at all. It's always in his mind but he will never again let it out.

Grace isn't sure what's happening. She doesn't seem to fully understand what has taken place. She's in a daze when they help her out of the truck and show her the burned out rubble that used to be her home. She cries and Madge cries with her. Grace hadn't realized how much she still had to lose: her mementos, her photographs, artwork and trinkets that had little meaning to anyone but an old woman who was slowly losing everything she once held dear. Furniture and appliances she could take or leave but how those mementos pulled at her heart.

When they go through the rubble, there's so little

they can salvage: a charred vase, some jewelry, a framed photograph. Each item comes with a memory and each is linked to countless other memories, fading memories of things lost. She puts them in a box and wonders how long she can keep going.

But she does keep going. She keeps going because she feels the love of her family. She keeps going because she believes, rightly or wrongly, that they need her. In some ways she supposes they have lost less than she has. It's her home and her memories. But they're young and she's old. They have their lives to live and it's her job to help them get on with it in any way she can.

The neighbors offer to take them in but they know there isn't enough room. They stay the night at the Bannister house. In the morning they look through the rubble one more time to see what they can save. There isn't much. Next to nothing at all. Madge finds a picture of me in a metal frame and a couple of charred books. That's it. Grace has lost everything. Madge holds her and they cry once more but she holds strong. As a child she has known her share of hard times – a sharecropper's daughter, an Oklahoma refugee, she's outlived everyone in her family but her dear sister, whom she might never see again. She worked most of her life and watched her husband and her oldest son die. She's prepared for anything life can throw at her. She says she's just happy that everyone is safe but she looks so tired. So tired. She's wondering how long she has left and how much more she can endure. She has been stronger than all of us for so long.

They go back to the military base only this time they're put up in one of the barracks – one of those shelters that looks like a giant barrel or tin can. There's plenty of room for their three families, each of which has children. They set them up as they had before only this time they are allowed go outside. They don't know why but the commander has changed his mind. Grace says he took one look at their long faces and felt for a moment what they were feeling. It seems some of them have hearts. Some of them have wives and children of their own. The neighborhood children are allowed to play with the military children and they all attend school on the base. It's taught by the parents but it's still school and they're grateful for it.

At any other time or at least before the fall Madge would be incensed. It's as if all the books they have and all the stories they know are biblical. It's like Sunday school five days a week. When had the Christian fundamentalists taken over the military? Maybe it happened a long time ago – during the modern day crusades that everyone keeps insisting was a war for democracy – and no one noticed.

When she asks one of the mothers about it (as delicately as she can manage) the woman just shrugs and says it's all they know. No one objects when Madge takes a turn teaching and tells the children a story out of the Great Depression: the westward migration of the Dust Bowl refugees. The children are fascinated by a story that comes so close to home. They draw pictures of old trucks and cars stacked with belongings, broken down on the long road west, bankers with police forcing people off their farms, people lining up for work, living in camps and sharing soup out of a large metal pot.

Some of the parents choke up when they recognize their own families and friends who had been pushed out of their homes by greedy bankers. It's as if they had lost that part of their own history. Everyone becomes so inwardly focused, so determined to survive within their small circles, that they refuse to see what's happening to everyone around them. They have forgotten that other people are their brothers and sisters. It sounds sophomoric but it's true: people everywhere are losing their sense of belonging to a greater community. At the same time they're developing a sense of community on a smaller scale. The military families on this base have their own community and the civilians have one at home – their neighborhood community.

That's something they had lost before hard times came. They lived in neighborhoods but they didn't really belong to them. If some misfortune struck a neighbor they might make a show of empathy but they felt no personal responsibility. They shrugged and went on with their lives, relieved that it was someone else. They paid taxes and relied on society to overcome hardships and rebuild broken lives. Now that there are no taxes to pay and no government agencies to come to their aid they're beginning to understand that they have to help each other if they want to survive.

They all help out in the schooling, the kitchen work, cleaning up and gardening. Whatever needs doing someone pitches in and they all do their share. Carlin proves resourceful repairing trucks and machinery. Grace takes an interest in the gardens where she's left pretty much alone to let her mind wander wherever it wants to go.

As that odd and wonderful man Albert Einstein discovered, time is a relative concept. Well, it is for Grace as she wanders the rows of fruits and vegetables, weeding, pruning, hoeing and mending fences. At some point she realizes her thoughts are leading her on the journey of her own life. It's then that she determines to write it all down. If she can leave nothing else, perhaps she can weave the story of her life, shaded of course by the bend of her memories and the singularity of her vision. She gathers up paper and pen – not so easy a task as it once was. It seems there's little demand these days and no one to manufacture items so little valued. She thinks and thinks, that first blank sheet of paper mocking her and goading her on, until she finally arrives at the word that sums it all up, nice and clean: Perseverance.

If it sounds harsh or crude she would be first to apologize but it's the only word that satisfies her sense of honesty and justice. She's not applying for sympathy though she would say it's a charity she rarely refuses. It's just that her life has been a series of hardships and there's no use denying it. She was born and raised in the hardship of a sharecropper's toil and it gave her an inheritance of strength. She was uprooted and displaced a dozen times before her tenth birthday and it gave her what her father called grit. She met and married her husband as they were both struggling to find their place in the world and it made them determined. She had walked the picket lines of a labor strike alongside her husband, raised her children through a decade of wanting, suffered through years of war, not knowing if her husband would return, and she never stopped long enough to give doubt a chance. She mourned deeply the sudden death of her first child and comforted her husband on his deathbed. Through it all she persevered.

She's a proud survivor and that's the gift she wishes to hand down to her grandchildren. She wants them each to know they come from good hardwood stock. Their people have lived through every hardship known to humankind. They had survived the great influenza epidemic, earthquakes and hurricanes, economic collapse and general misfortune.

*We have always overcome. We have never given up. We are a family of survivors.*

Perhaps she wants to remind herself as well as her family. It's comforting. She was not on the front lines of the Great War or at the back of the line in the Great Depression but she knows what they were. She remembers. She remembers the trembling in her mother's embrace, the lines of worry on her rugged face, and the tears that threatened to emerge from her father's proud eyes. One never forgets the little things, the common things that seem so small and unimportant but in the end tell us everything that matters.

The hard times that have knocked us back on our heels and made us wonder how we manage to get up every morning do not last forever. We survive and like the poet says it makes us stronger. She only wishes it will make us wiser as well.

It's not as if this is the first time our economy had collapsed like an overloaded truck with a blown tire. Each time it's the same story. A select group of elite businessmen on Wall Street think they are above the law of gravity. Governed by greed they buy the politicians so they can operate on their own terms. It took JP Morgan to save us the first time and Franklin Roosevelt to pull us back from the brink in the thirties and forties. You'd think we would have learned but you'd be wrong. Again and again we allow greed to govern greed as we march straight over an economic cliff. So it seems we never quite acquire the knowledge we need to prevent the fall but we do acquire the lesson of perseverance. We survive.

It may be the hardest lesson to learn, especially when you're young and so full of drama, when the universe evolves around you and every moment is celluloid – or so it seems. Grace was young once, so long ago even the memories are worn, but she knows well the depths of the human soul. She knows how hard it can be to walk out the door and how difficult to ask for help. She knows that for most of us there is help waiting to be asked. This is what she wants the young ones to learn. They have a family and a community that is yearning to help and nurture them even if they don't always know it. We will survive. We will persevere and thrive. It's the way of our people.

Grace loves the gardens. The greenhouses are so regimental and orderly. They lack a woman's touch. They have no flair, no style and no sense of the aesthetic. The camp is in command of the greenhouses but the families are in charge of the gardens. For most people in these troubled times there's no more room for the aesthetic. There's no water or soil for roses and lilies and petunias. But here at the base there's plenty to eat. They yield a surplus that they distribute to the local communities. So they allow their wives the indulgence of growing flowers and the flowers are in bloom. Grace breathes them in and lavishes them with attention. She sings to them and recites poetry about the beauty of nature, the lost arts, and the diminishing value of creativity. She learns new poems so that the flowers won't grow bored with the mad ramblings of an old woman. She thinks she will live the remainder of her life at the base and she will be content to spend her final days in these beautiful gardens with the last glorious flowers upon the earth but it is not to be.

She misses the arts. She can't count how many times she suggests that they start a theater. They always humor her with a nod a smile and then they go about their business. There's always far too much to worry about, too many plans and emergencies, to devote one's time to frivolous activities. Madge is sympathetic of course but even Grace understands her resistance. She's unwilling to entertain the notion that they might not leave this place for a very long time. She's pleasant and giving to everyone around her but beneath the surface she's suffering. She hates this place. Even after they move out of the warehouse it's far too cold and impersonal for Madge. She does not want her kids to grow up in a military environment. She also expects her husband to return and she worries I will not be able to find them here. No one can find them here.

She never says these things aloud of course. She holds them inside. It's not in her nature to criticize other people for who they are. She reserves her judgment for what people do and these people are kind to her family. Of course they were not so kind to the criminals who invaded their neighborhood. That's another thing that holds her beneath a shadow. She doesn't believe they deserved to be killed. When Carlin confirms her suspicions the darkness of knowing that they are all in some way complicit in a massacre falls over her. They all feel it but Madge feels it as a mother feels the pain of her child.

It's strange how they all push it from their minds. What did they think would happen? How could they not know? But they didn't know or at least they guided that knowledge to the back of their minds where they would never have to look at it – or so they thought. But we always have to look – even if we wait until our dying day. Each and every one of us holds some responsibility for a horrible event – one that we would never sanction or defend but one that we might have prevented but for whatever reason did not. The other side of it of course is that some if not most of her own community would undoubtedly have died. Some of the women would surely have been raped and many of them would have been terribly wounded if they had chosen to fight on their own. On the other hand, if they had chosen to give them what they asked for and they asked for no more than they needed, then tragedy might have been averted. *What if* is a fool's game but it haunts her and will not leave her in peace.

Who can say? We are only human. We act more out of raw instinct, out of fear and prejudice, than we do out of reasoned deliberation. That we are guilty to some degree of acting too swiftly, of presuming too much, is beyond doubt. These are the kind of questions they should have asked before they summoned the cavalry but they did not. This is what brings tears to the soul of considerate and decent human beings. It should have torn at theirs perhaps far more than it had. Perhaps they were just too close to take in all sides of the equation. There are the children to consider. Even Madge could not get by that consideration. The children come first and no risks can be taken that puts them in danger.

They survived and the children are safe. In the end it's all that matters. That's what people do. We move on. We do not dwell on what might have been. We take those steps that will ensure we will not have to face such choices again.

The weather turns warmer and the rains begin to fall. You smell it before you see it: life struggling to be reborn. They had stayed longer than they expected and Madge is beginning to worry that the children are becoming attached. How many times can they be uprooted without doing harm? It's a way of life for so many people – men, women and children alike – but she doesn't want it to happen to Denim and Charlie. Children need security and families need a home.

One evening after dinner Carlin clears his throat, narrows his eyes and announces that he believes the time has come to go back home and rebuild. Madge is so relieved and happy she cries and gives him a hug. It's the first sign that her brother is looking forward since the massacre. Madge can tell that Joan is disappointed but she doesn't say so. She likes the base. She likes the fact that they're taken care of and they're safe but even she recognizes what it means for Carlin and the family. They need him. They depend on him. The children need a father and they all need a strong man. Uncle Bud isn't up to the job. He's a fun loving man, funny and pleasant and willing, but he's old and feeble. He and Aunt Mildred look older every day.

Carlin talks to their information officer who talks to his commander. The word comes back that they want the family to consider staying. Some of the military families have grown attached and want them to join their community and the commander wants the men to sign on as soldiers. He wants Carlin in particular. It might have been tempting but after Carlin had seen them in action, after what he had witnessed, it's not possible. The other neighborhood families decide to stay so they say their goodbyes and pack their things.

The military does right by them. They load up a second truck with cut lumber, tools, nails and screws, coils of wire and various supplies, a new generator and a ten-gallon jug of gas. No one is quite sure why they treat the family so well but they do. Maybe they know how Carlin feels and maybe they want to make it up to him in some perverted way. It doesn't matter any more. They thank their hosts and count their blessings.

The gardens and peach blossoms are in bloom on the day they leave. It's early morning, the magpies and crows are out in force and the birds of spring are singing. The air is crisp and moist. Everything seems to breathe possibilities and the kind of love that urges you on dances in their hearts. It's a good life and a good day to remember why.

They ride to the old neighborhood not knowing what tomorrow will bring but they are willing to believe it will all be well. They're alive, together and determined to stay that way. When they arrive home they find a bearded man in well-traveled clothes with a walking stick and a dog sitting on the porch where Grace's home once stood. Grace wonders aloud why the neighbors would let a bum and his mangy dog squat on their porch. But it's not a bum.

It takes a good long moment for them to recognize me. I've come home.

## THE REUNION

If it is possible to lift a cloud of sorrow in a single moment it happened that day.

It seems as though a lifetime has passed between our parting and reunion and maybe it has as the length and strength of our embrace bears witness. It's like Penelope greeting her lost adventurer Odysseus or Tristan finally returning to his beloved Isolde only it's real and it's happening before our weary, tear stained eyes. We stand before the wreckage of our former home and share tears of joy.

I promise Madge a dozen times during the course of the evening that I will never leave the family again. When I catch my breath and everyone settles down I relate the experience of my travels, the people I have met and the communities that welcomed me – almost as if they are family. I share my dream of uniting these communities for mutual benefit. I go on for what seems like hours until only Madge remains to listen. I remember why I fell in love with her in the first place. She shares my passion. When someone has that kind of passion you either follow or walk away. It doesn't matter whether it's a good idea or a bad one you just follow and hope for the best.

I tell her all about the people I met on my journey and the communities they've created. I tell her about the special bonds I formed with the college students at the Sun Camp, their development of sustainable energy systems, watering systems, farming and security. It's unfortunate that they found it necessary but they had begun building walls and lookout stations to defend their community from outsiders. She relates what happened here in the neighborhood and we both understand that every community must do the same. But we should also form alliances with the surrounding neighborhoods and the other communities to increase our diversity, expand our pool of talent and strengthen our defenses.

It's an awkward time in many ways. The family has just returned to rebuild their home and I'm asking them to consider much, much more – a grand plan on a larger scale. We need schools and community centers and a master plan to develop our resources. We need some form of government and trade agreements and communications. I'm asking them to rebuild society from the ground up, one brick at a time, and strangely enough it seems to make sense to everyone I talk with.

I find it comforting that I'm not alone in my thinking. I'm not just a dreamer making plans that no one will ever carry out. It all makes sense.

Madge and I take a sleeping bag and go off to be alone, leaving Grace with the children. It's a wonderful night, serenaded by the moon and entertained by the muses of forgotten mythology. There's music and dance and stories full of laughter around a makeshift campfire. It's a night when dreams play out their most fanciful tunes and angels in the heavens look down on us with bemused approval.

Grace looks on with the pride of a mother and a smile that will not stop giving. She will never forget this night for as long or as briefly as she should live. She only wishes her husband was here to witness it. He would have taken such pleasure in the festivities. He loved a celebration and he would have loved to see the children so happy. It's a glorious night and one that the family will store in a box of treasures for as long as we survive. It is so important to hold on to these moments for that is what sustains us when times are hard.

And then it rains. The sky breaks open and floods us with tears of joy. The tents the military commander had provided them prove sound as we all sleep to the drumbeat of raindrops over our heads. Madge and I find shelter in a storage shed but in the morning we arise fresh, full of life and eager to get to work.

The entire neighborhood seems to share our enthusiasm. Not only do we have a home to build, we make plans for a community center that can serve as a schoolhouse and a hub for a textile industry. We make plans to start our own hemp crop. People from the neighborhood are organizing and dividing into work crews.

Even Carlin gets caught up in it. I miss him more than I imagined I would and maybe he feels the same. He needs someone to help take the pressure off. If he's honest he would have to admit that he resents how my ideas carry more weight than his but he has the decency to keep it to himself. We don't see eye to eye on a lot of things but in our time apart we have learned to respect each other. Oh, we still have our disagreements. He considers my ideas about uniting with the other communities impractical and hopelessly idealistic. Carlin figures we have enough to think about right here but even he agrees some of my ideas have merit. He can't deny that other communities have skills and resources the neighborhood doesn't have and if there's another threat to security the communities could band together and do what has to be done. We wouldn't have to call in the authorities. We wouldn't have to witness another massacre. Hopefully, we could handle it ourselves.

Sure it makes sense. We have some rebuilding to do here and now and maybe the others can help. Down the road we can return the favor.

It makes even more sense when Sugar brings a crew over from the Bridge Camp. He takes a look at what's going on and he knows we need help - a lot of help. Carlin's doing the best he can but he has no concept of building. I don't feel I can intervene without bumping heads but Sugar can. The way he puts it: *You have this guy telling everyone what to do when he doesn't know how to tie his own shoes.* Enough said.

Sugar takes the initiative as only he can and Carlin steps aside without a fight.

The bridge crew helps out as good neighbors with no expectation of a return on their efforts but it comes to pass that the neighborhood has some things that they can use. For one they have a couple of industrial sized ovens that can be put to use baking bricks and roofing tiles. After all they'd been through Carlin and his friends put in some time and effort making weapons too and what they came up with is extremely effective.

Some people are afraid of snakes. Sugar is afraid of needles. When they show him their air gun with darts treated with some kind of tranquilizer it sends a bad case of shivers running straight through him. They say it can put a runaway mountain lion down so you can imagine what it would do to a man. Stop him cold and lay him out. One man takes it and the rest run like rabbits. No more security problems.

Sugar has to hand it to these city boys. They did this one right. The Bridge Camp will still put up their walls because they figure it's just a matter of time before the criminal element comes at them with heavy artillery no matter what the consequences. The neighborhood has their share of guns and bombs stashed away but they're determined not to use them. We figure that's the difference between them and us: With them it's a matter of time. With us it's a matter of conscience.

Once things are reasonably organized and the work is under way, I want to make a run to recruit more workers, planners, carpenters and solar engineers but Madge is petrified and I won't go without her blessing. She's afraid if I leave they'll never see me again. I make the point that it has to be me. If it's anyone else it might not be safe. After all that has happened with the gangs and the criminals everyone is a little touchy. There's a feeling that no one can be trusted. Madge finally agrees to let me go on the condition that she will go with me. I put up a fight but it's no use. She has her mind made up and that's that. We go back and forth for days before I finally relent. Grace, Carlin and Joan agree to take care of the kids and off we go: Me and Madge and my loyal dog Cinn.

We don't know it at the time but Denim will take off after us. By the time they figure out he's missing the day is pretty much gone. Carlin says he'll be all right but Joan and Grace are nearly hysterical. Denim was left in their care and they dropped the ball. Carlin can't argue with that. The boy is their responsibility and if anything happens to him the blame will fall squarely on his shoulders.

Carlin goes after us, heading for the Bridge Camp, figuring we'll at least check in there before moving on. If luck is on his side, we would spend the night and he'll be able to find Denim so we can all talk some sense into him and Carlin will take him back home.

It's strange moving through the streets at night. Eerie. There are fires all over town, metal barrels in the middle of streets circled by people, children and adults, eyes shining with firelight, more fearful than menacing.

Carlin tries to stay in the shadows as much as possible, moving swiftly and with a purpose, never stopping to talk or attract attention. People are unaccustomed to anyone but prowlers and criminals traveling at night. He's afraid with good cause but without provocation and he's worried that Denim is out there somewhere. He's a good kid and very able. He's smart in both the street and book learning ways. He can take care of himself. But if a grown man is afraid on these streets at night, how is it for a boy? It's wet hot and he's covered in sticky sweat by the time he reaches the bridge. Unfortunately, we have been there only briefly and there's no sign of Denim.

Carlin thinks about tracking us down the road but the people at the bridge persuade him it's far too dangerous. Sugar convinces him it's best if he stays the night. He says: *Nothing good can come of someone else getting lost out there chasing shadows and ending up bruised and beaten by some gang of ragtag ruffians.* He's certain that if Denim has only half the good sense his father has he'll be just fine. In fact, he says: *He's probably hunkering down by a campfire with his mother and father right now.* He gives Carlin a wink and that's all the assurance he needs. He stays the night and heads back home the next morning. Something about that wink and the way Sugar talks about the situation gives him confidence everything will turn out okay.

He catches hell from Joan and Grace, of course, but everything will turn out fine.

Three or four days pass before word finally arrives that Denim is okay. Someone sent a crawler to let the family know he's with his parents and they've decided to continue their journey with him. They will take every precaution and they will return safely in due time. It's a great relief to everyone but especially to Carlin. Not an hour had gone by without a discussion of whose fault it is that Denim slipped out and whether or not Carlin should still be on the road looking for him. It was getting to the point where he couldn't take it any more. He feels bad enough as it is.

# BUILDING ALLIANCES

No one is happier or more relieved when I finally returned home than my son Denim. As much as he thinks of his father, that little he thinks of his Uncle Carlin – admittedly with some cause. As long as I've known him Carlin has had some underlying inferiority complex that leads him to pretend he always knows what he's doing even when it becomes painfully obvious that he doesn't.

Denim sees the truth straight away. He senses that others feel the same but no one wants to say the obvious. I'm proud of my son but I also know it's not his place to question Carlin's authority. He's just a boy, even if he's right. It seems I've come home at a good time, a time when I have something to offer the community, including giving my brother-in-law some needed relief.

The neighborhood work crews are a disaster. Sugar and his crew came to lend a hand but Sugar was reluctant to step in and take charge. It's not his place. Carlin had all these committees in charge of projects but it seems the only thing that comes off as planned are the parties they hold every night. They have a lot of music, dance and homemade brew but the only ones who get up to work the next day are the Bridge crews. Even the kids know it's no way to get anything done.

Sugar tries to talk some sense into him but Carlin always has an excuse. It keeps the workers' spirits up. It breaks the tension of a day's labor. It takes the edge off. It gives the men something to get up for every day.

So every night the Bridge crew retires early, gets up at dawn and goes to work while the neighborhood crews sleep off their hangovers. After two or three weeks the neighborhood workers start following the Bridge crew's lead, skipping the nightly festivities and retiring early, and it has an immediate impact.

Denim doesn't miss a thing. His eyes and ears are always open and tuned to the issues of the day. I often try to see things though his eyes. At his age I hadn't seen half the hardship and struggle that Denim has – except on TV and it's not the same. He thinks Uncle Carlin wants to replace me and it makes him mad – madder than he should be. It's not Carlin's fault he had to step up and be the man of the family. More than once I take Denim aside and try to explain that if anyone is to blame it's me but he still has a hard time understanding.

One of the reasons he ran off after us is he can't stand the idea of having to listen to Carlin boss people around. He says it's like being in the Boy Scouts or the army: *Yes sir! Yes sir!*

He knows what he's doing when he follows after us. People said it was dangerous and it is but he and his friends have been all over town before and after dark. He isn't sure if his mom knows it or thinks it's okay. She knows he can take care of himself. He's heard her tell Joan: *I'm not going to put a leash on him!*

His mom thought he stopped going with her to look

167

for me because it made him sad. He tells me he went off looking on his own. He probably would have found me too but he and the boys were afraid to go anywhere near the bridge. They'd heard stories that there was no one but killers and thieves living there and for some reason he believed it. I set the record straight, telling him and anyone who asks that the people under the bridge are no different than you or I. They just had a little less luck when hard times hit. They didn't have another house to go to so they did what they had to do.

Denim caught up to us at the Bridge Camp. Unfortunately, we didn't know that at the time. We had a hunch he might follow so we stayed around long enough to have a cold drink and talk a while. When he didn't show up we hit the road.

As we would soon find out, Denim was there, hanging back in the shadows and staying just out of sight. He follows along until we hook up with a solar crawler down a long country road. You have to jog a little to keep up with a crawler when it's rolling but the thing keeps going as long as the sun shines and then some. Solar technology is getting better and better at storing energy. At the rate we're going it won't be long before we can run a crawler all night long if we want. But at this stage we take what we can get.

He follows us for maybe five miles before we pull over for a lunch break. He hunches over down the road to keep an eye on us and think things through. He decides he'd better come clean, figuring he might be able to stay up with us for the rest of the day but then again he might not. We're already a good distance from home so he decides to take a chance. Getting stuck out here alone after nightfall is not an experience he wants to test thank God.

# HARD TIMES

I'll never forget the sight of him. He stands up and walks down the road as if it's the most natural thing in the world, just a boy on a stroll in the countryside. Standing before us words escape him until finally he stammers, eyes fixed to the toes of his tennis shoes, that he wants to go with us. His mother doesn't hesitate. She opens her arms for a hug and tells him how glad she is to see him. She tells me she thinks it's a great idea. I take a harder stand for his own good.

*We ought to turn this crawler around right now and get you back to town before sunset! Sugar can put you to work.*

Denim stands there with his mouth open as his mom and I argue back and forth the reasons for taking him with us against the reasons for taking him back. Madge says he's grown up a lot while I was away. He's capable and mature for his age. I concede I can see that but he has violated a trust. How can we rely on a boy who won't do as he's told? Madge counters that it's only his desire to be with his parents that made him disobey. He's a good boy, strong and reliable, and he proves it time and again. I don't doubt it and maybe I'd have done the same when I was his age.

When I finally cave, Denim breathes a sigh of relief. I tell him he can go along as long as he pulls his weight and doesn't complain any more than we do. Denim promises on his mother's grave and we have a good laugh about that. What about my grave?

The truth is we're proud of him for taking the initiative. Though neither of us will say it out loud, it's exactly what we hoped he would do. When I first talked about making this trip, I wanted to go alone. I thought it was too dangerous to risk anyone else. Madge was determined to go with me and wouldn't take no for an answer.

At some point I said: *Well, if you're going why don't we take Denim and Charlie? Keep the whole family together!* I said it with an ironic grin but I gave Denim a look like maybe he *could* go, maybe he should if he's old enough and smart enough to handle it. We knew Charlie was too young but we both thought Denim was capable if he was willing to take the initiative.

When we said goodbye I pulled him aside and told him: *Son, if you ever need to know where we're going, if something happens where you need to know, Sugar can show you the way.* I wanted him to know I trusted Sugar more than anyone in town aside from his mother, even more that Carlin. So he had an idea where we were going if he had the guts to follow. We never said so but we thought he knew. It was in his spirit. He didn't care what people said. He didn't care how dangerous they told him it was. To Denim it was a chance to go somewhere and see how other people lived. He couldn't wait. If we took him back, he probably would have followed us again. We'd have had to tie him down to stop him.

We all climb on the crawler and head on down the road. We let Denim drive until he gets bored which is soon enough because it goes so slow. We count crows. There must be a million of them. Like ants and roaches, crows seem to thrive in hard times. Little wonder. They're smarter than most people and more adaptable.

We play games and talk about anything and everything that enters our minds. When we come across other people, walking or driving a crawler or some other vehicle, we get quiet and pay attention. Some people make you think twice. You can see they're sizing you up, wanting to scare you into keeping your distance. Most people are nice though, smiling and saying hello as we crawl by. Some of them have kids around Denim's age. We would've liked to visit and let them play but we didn't want to slow down. Places to go and things to do. People are counting on us.

When the sun goes down we pitch a tent and make a fire a little ways off the road. Usually we find a place where people have already camped. I have a good idea where these places are. I've been down this road and I know a lot of the people who live and travel here.

The first night at camp I tell them the story of when I found Cinnamon - or when she found me. Cinn beams. She knows I'm talking about her. She's a smart dog - always warning me when something is out of line. Every time we come across a suspicious looking character she growls real low to put us on alert. I tell Denim she's smarter than I am but he doesn't think so. He says I'm smart enough to take her on and she's smart enough to stick with me. We're a good match for each other. I can't argue with that.

Madge says that's how things are supposed to be: give and take. Problems come up when someone takes more than they give and you should think twice when someone offers you something for nothing. Nine out of ten times it's a bad deal.

Cinn and Denim become especially good friends on our trip. Madge and I are often busy talking to people and making plans. So Cinn tags along with Denim as they explore the surroundings. He wonders if Cinn is short for Cindy but I tell him it stands for Cinnamon from a song I know. The people out at the Sun Camp played it for us and Cinn jumped up and danced along.

171

She knows it's her song.

She's a good dog. The best. Time and again, I find myself looking at her, studying her, admiring the way she carries herself. Any way you want to look at it I'm lucky to have found her. Some people in the neighborhood wanted me to put her on a leash but I refused. She's as free as I am and always will be. I did give her a blue bandana to wear around her neck and she seems to like that. Dogs like to have something that lets people know they're special.

Our first stop on the third day out is The Farm. Leon and Margie take us in, feed us and treat us like family. Everyone is friendly except for Mr. Connelly, the Boss Man, of course. Cinn recognizes him from before and growls every time she sees him. I explain to Denim that we have some history together. I tell him he was the boss before things changed and I was a part of the change. I explain that he made a profit from working people like slaves.

*He made a lot of money off the sweat of honest workers.*

Denim squints and asks what I mean by that. How do you explain to a nine-year-old the harsh realities of unfettered capitalism? How do you explain the greed of people who want far more than they need, more than they could ever need? Madge weighs in explaining we all used to work for money instead of rations or credits. She explains that a business would hire you to do a job. Then they took the money you made from that job and gave the worker some of the money. The business kept the rest.

Denim thinks about this for a long time. There's no such thing as real money any more. People still have it and some people collect it and guard it like a treasure but it isn't worth much. There are still board games that have play money and the idea is you take as much as you can get. Whoever has the most money wins the game. It can be fun but it's just a game. It's a strange way to run the real world in the eyes of a child. He likes it better when the people who work get the credits. We make sure he knows that we feel the same way.

The people at The Farm work hard every day, raising the crops, taking care of the animals, building the cabins they live in, making repairs and keeping everything in working order. They cook their own meals and see to it that no one is hungry and everyone is as comfortable as possible with what they have. Everyone seems happy with the new situation – everyone but the Boss Man.

Denim gets to play with the Boss Man's kids a couple times but they really aren't much fun. They don't like to get dirty. They like indoor games like his mom does. She says we can learn a lot of good lessons from the right kind of games. Denim likes checkers but he'd rather be out playing any time.

One of the Boss Man's kids is a girl named Rachel. She's cute as a puppy and Denim is just the age when a pretty girl catches his eye. She likes Denim too and asks him one afternoon if he wants to kiss her. He tells her no way but then he starts thinking about it. He's seen guys kissing girls back home. They seem to like it. He thinks it makes them kind of stupid but the next time she asks he says why not. He kisses her right in the open. Unfortunately Rachel's mom sees it all and that's the end of playtime with the boss's kids. It isn't a big deal because there are other kids to play with in the camp. They'd taken them in since the big change took place. Denim says he doesn't miss Rachel but we know he does. Every once in a while we'll catch him looking at the big white house, trying to catch a glimpse of the little girl who gave him his first kiss.

It seems to him his mother and I are way too serious and don't have much time to look after him and even less time to play. We talk to people about what they need to make things better. I have my notebook and I'm always writing in it. There are a lot of drawings and lists but there are also stories about the people we meet and the different ways they get by. I've written about Denim and Charlie and Madge and Sugar and Leon and the people of the Sun Camp.

I let Denim look at it from time to time but I always stop him before he gets too far. I don't want to mold his point of view. I want him to come to his own conclusions. I tell him it's a private matter but I hope someday he'll read it all and tell me what he thinks. I tell him I hope he'll collect stories himself some day. He seems to like that idea and starts his own notebook, making a point to write or draw something almost every day.

When I introduce Denim to Leon I realize how few people of color were in our lives before the fall. I don't know why. I've always known people of different races and cultures but our circle of friends looked very much as we do. It is something I hope will change in the new order though I fear it won't. There's a chance it will only get worse. We need to find ways to interact with all kinds of people. We need to make a point of it. If we don't, we'll go right back to the ways of prejudice: us against them.

Leon will become one of the first men of color my son will hold up as a role model. I tell him we're good friends and Leon is the leader of this place. I admire his character and I sense Denim feels the same. Madge and I spend most of our time with Leon and his partner Margie. They get along well. Madge tells Denim that Leon and I look at things with the same eyes. He thinks that's strange until I explain that Leon feels the same way I do on things that matter.

Denim makes friends with a kid about his age named Juan and they're always off on adventures. It's good to see him having fun and making friends with different kinds of people, people he might not have met before hard times came. There isn't much that goes on that Juan and Denim don't know about. We leave them to their own as long as they stay out of trouble and explain things the best we can whenever he asks. He asks often.

There are problems brewing at The Farm. You can feel it. You see it in the workers' eyes and the way they carry themselves, looking around as if they expect some enemy to confront them. Leon won't admit it but if you ask he's a little afraid of Connelly. He says the man is trying like hell to get rid of him because he blames us for everything that's happened. Lately the he's made some threats about taking control and kicking the dead weight out. Leon is about ready to take matters into his own hands.

*Burn that damn house down!*

I advise caution. I know how he feels, of course, but you don't start a war unless you know how it will turn out. The only thing we know for sure is that a lot of good people will be hurt or killed. It's the last thing we need. I tell him I have a plan and ask him to give it a chance.

After supper we call everyone together. Leon has warned me that there are spies and stooges among them but I want all the workers present. I identify the traitors and tell them straight up I know that Connelly has recruited them to cause trouble and break up any attempt to organize the workers into a united group. I tell them I know what they're up to and it isn't going to work.

A bald-headed man shouts out: *Who appointed you to speak for anyone?*

I reply: *We'll find out in a little while who I speak for but we all know who you speak for!*

Everybody who isn't a Boss Man stooge nods in acknowledgement. They all know I speak the truth. I announce we're going to have a vote and that everyone will be expected to honor the vote. *If you don't agree you can leave now.* The stooges don't like the sound of it but all they can do is grumble like a mob of fools. We have a contract typed up that spells it all out: the workers will have a say on who gets hired and who gets fired. It spells out their right to negotiate and to share in the profits – not profits in the old sense, not currency, but mostly in the form of trading credits. The Boss Man has his own network of trading partners and he uses his credits to get everything from fuel and generators to fancy clothes and perfume for his wife. He's a hoarder and he has more than his share of gold and currency as well. That will come to an end.

*It's simple and to the point: You're either for the union or against, in it or out.*

We pass out pencils and squares of paper to every worker with instructions to vote yes or no. *A yes means you want a union and want to join it. A no means you don't want any part of it.* We give them time to talk it over and wait for everyone to mark their votes. Then we gather them up and count them one by one. After a while it's pretty clear how the vote will turn out but we count them all. The union wins by a near unanimous vote. It's everyone against the stooges.

Next they choose representatives to lead the union. Leon is elected president. It's a victory for the working people. It's the kind of victory we rarely experienced in our lives before the breakdown. Unions had all but vanished and workers did what they were told without question or complaint. If you caused problems you didn't have a job.

The next day we all go together to meet with Boss Man Connelly in the big house. We don't ask for his consent. We tell him how it's going to be. He will receive 25% of the profit which seems more than fair. It's more than enough to enable him and his family to live in comfort. We give him the contract and tell him he can sign or not sign. It doesn't matter. No one will work at The Farm if they don't join the union. Even the boss's stooges sign on. Connelly looks like his head will explode but he doesn't say a word. He just mumbles something indecipherable and nods to indicate he understands.

That night we build a big fire and have a celebration. There's lots of food with cakes and cookies and music and dancing and laughing and hollering. It's great fun for the kids. They run around like free souls doing whatever they feel like doing so long as they don't get into trouble. Denim says it's a lot more fun than the parties they have back home. Madge tells him these people have music in their souls. Denim asks her if he has music in his soul and he looks a little worried when she doesn't answer straight away. She looks him in the eyes for a spell, as if she's looking past all the wrong things he ever did or said, and tells him he has as much music in his soul as anyone else. She says it's up to him to keep it that way.

We leave in the morning, feeling fresh and invigorated, right after breakfast. Denim likes The Farm and he knows we like it too so he asks us why we have to go. Madge tells him we're on a great adventure and what kind of adventure would it be if we stay the first place we come to? Denim can't argue with that even though he wouldn't have a problem if we decided to stay. I tell him he'll like the next place we're going almost as much or maybe even more. I tell him there are kids there too and the whole place is run by young people. Denim asks if there's music there. I wink and say: *Son, one thing I've learned is that there's music everywhere you go.*

It's a long haul to the Sun Camp. We have to camp out three nights before we arrive. Denim isn't used to camping out in the country. There are animals out here he's never heard or seen. Cinn growls to announce their presence and barks if they get close to camp.

We listen and identify them: hoot owls, raccoons, possums, coyotes and a couple of mountain lions. There are wild dogs and a lot of crows everywhere we go. I tell him the crows will be here long after we're gone. They're like cockroaches with brains. I have a lot of respect for those animals and I want Denim to know he can learn a lot by watching them.

The mountain lions can be scary when you're out there under the stars at night. They've retained their fear of humans but it dissipates by the day. They used to stay up in the mountains but now they come down to the towns and cities. Without guns and ammunition, people don't kill the big cats like they used to.

I tell Denim that we shouldn't be too afraid because we have these dart guns that Carlin's friends came up with. The darts are treated with a chemical that's supposed to be powerful enough to knock a big animal down without killing it – or a human for that matter. Denim isn't too sure how well it will work because half the things Carlin and his friends worked out don't work at all. I'm afraid I feel the same way.

We camp off the road and keep the fire down so no one can see us. We have to be more cautious with Denim here. Even Cinn stays quiet. I talk about how things have changed since the first time I went down this road. It's safer now because the people from the Sun Camp and other places I don't know much about are patrolling it. They keep the road clear and make repairs. The first time I traveled this road there were old rusted out cars abandoned here. We cleared them out so we could make better time and used the parts and materials to make and repair machines. We try to recycle everything we use. There are no more factories and you can't send off for parts from a catalogue anymore. You learn to make do with what you have.

Twice I see people I know going the other way on crawlers. They tell us that everything's fine at the Sun Camp and they're waiting for us.

On the second night we have to put the fire out and stay quiet while some people in a truck, yelling and whooping, drive by. I tuck Cinn under my arm and whisper for her to be quiet. They pass by without noticing us but it gives Denim a scare. It's a reminder that there are still dangerous people in the world and you have to be careful.

On the third day we turn off on a dirt road and crawl up the hill to the camp. We stop to put a flag up and let the people at the camp know we're on our way.

We're bone tired when we arrive but they welcome us with smiles and hugs. Zar is anxious to show me the projects they've started and completed and the progress they've made in my absence. He takes me on a tour while Madge and Denim sit down to eat, rest and socialize. I'm amazed at what they've accomplished and I hope Madge and Denim will be as impressed as I am. Madge knows this is where I want us to settle but we haven't shared that thought with the children.

Most of the kids here are younger than Denim but there are two boys and two girls that are about his age. The boys are named Boz and Phoenix. The girls are Cloud and River. Denim thinks they're cute. Two boys and two girls means that he's the guy without a dance partner and that's exactly what Boz tells him.

Stubborn like his father, he won't admit it but it unsettles him. It makes him want to prove his new friend wrong. Not that he had ever danced with a girl before but it doesn't sit well that he's the one left out of anything. He's at the age when boys start thinking about girls. River is pretty and sweet. She's Phoenix's sister and she's no girly girl. She keeps up with the boys and isn't afraid to get dirty. Cloud is a little younger and a little less the tomboy but she likes to run around with them. Denim hadn't known a lot of girls who didn't act like girls. He thinks they're cool.

Naturally the minute Denim decides he likes River, Cloud decides she likes Denim. Why does it always seem to work that way? Human nature I guess: Wanting what we can't have. Back home that would have thrown Denim off his game but this is a different kind of place so he decides to go with it. It turns out Cloud's the best girl he ever met. She loves Cinn and they start hanging out together most of the time. She shows Denim where they made a pond in the creek and how they were turning out electricity from running water. She shows him where they make solar panels and explains that they take light from the sun and turn it into power.

The solar assembly plant is exceptionally clean and they have to be careful not to touch anything or even breathe on it. She shows him another place where they make solar crawlers. Some of the crawlers are getting too fast for their name. They're made of bike wheels and lightweight aluminum. I suggest they should start calling them solar cruisers.

After a few days it becomes clear Denim is falling in love with the Sun Camp and Madge is not far behind. They love the sense of belonging fostered by gathering together in the community room for every meal and every decision of importance. Madge loves that they're nearly self-sufficient and earth friendly. The food is excellent even though they don't eat meat, explaining to the children that it's wasteful to feed good food to animals only to turn animals into food.

Madge gets involved with schooling the children and Denim remarks: *It's not boring like it is back home.* They learn everything they need to know about how things work and how to build things and how to make electricity from wind, running water and the sun. They learn about renewable energy and how to stop poisoning the planet we live on.

Denim never thought he'd say it but school is just all right and they still have plenty of time to play. The camp believes playing is just as important as reading and writing. The kids can't agree more. But they like the books they read too. Everything about the place is good and fair and interesting. They make a point of finding out where a child's interests are as well as the child's abilities. They use a child's interests to guide his or her education.

Even when Denim gets in a fight with Boz because he doesn't like how he treats Cloud things turn out okay. We get together with Boz and his parents and work things out. Denim understands why Boz is mad and Boz understands why he's mad and they both understand there are better ways to handle their disagreements than to fight over it. They only need to talk about it. They shake hands and become good friends again – maybe better than they were before.

Madge and I think Cloud and Denim are amusing but we keep an eye on them. They're having fun and learning things at the same time. Cloud's parents don't get mad like the Connelly's did when they find out Denim kissed their daughter. He liked it. They both did. They made a vow not to tell anyone about it but someone snitched them off.

Denim never found out who it was. It's not a big deal because we don't make it a big deal. Cloud's parents tell them they should be careful not to push it too far. Denim knows what they're talking about and all he can say is forget about it. He and Cloud both understand that's just what parents are supposed to say in a situation like that. They're kids but they aren't stupid.

After a while Denim decides he likes the Sun Camp better than any other place. It's better than The Farm and better than the Bridge Camp and a whole lot better

182

than back home with Carlin and the family. He knows better than to say it out loud. He loves his grandma as much as he loves anyone but she's not like she used to be. It isn't her fault she can't remember things. He loves Aunt Joan and her kids even if they are spoiled brats. He likes Uncle Bud and Aunt Mildred and even Carlin isn't as bad as he used to think he was. His mother explained why he's the way he is and Denim sort of understands it's not his fault either. It's just the way things are. Still, if he has his choice, this is the place he wants to live. Like his mom said to Holly, it's a great place to raise kids.

One night after dinner in the community room, we walk back to our cabin and get set up for the evening when Denim asks straight up: *Why can't we live here?* We look at each other and smile before I reply: *We can and we're giving it some thought.* He doesn't push his luck. He really expects us to say our place is back home with the family. It puts a smile on his face to think we might end up at the Sun Camp after all. It puts a smile on our faces as well.

One of the things Denim likes most about the Sun Camp is the music. It seems like half the people in camp play the guitar and the other half plays the drums. All the kids either dance or play drums too. We sit around in a big circle every Friday night. Someone plays every night but the big circle is on Friday. There are a couple of fiddles and flutes and a handful of harmonicas. It doesn't matter if you know how to play, you learn. It doesn't matter if you have someone to dance with you just get out there and dance.

We take part in three circles and I've never seen Denim have so much fun. He tells us it's the best time he's ever had.

We have a big music circle the night before we have to leave. Denim doesn't want to leave and he doesn't think we want to either but it's time. We have to get back because people count on us. There's business that has to get done and if we're going to make the move, we have to get Charlie.

We say our goodbyes after breakfast and head out. We get on a solar train with four crawlers linked together. Two other couples are going with us.

All the kids run out to see us off and Cloud looks a little sad. Denim whispers in her ear: *Don't worry we'll be back.* She replies: *You promise?* And he says *yes.* That puts a smile on her sweet young face. Boz and Phoenix and River and Cloud follow us all the way down the road to the flagpole. Then we wave goodbye again and go on our way.

One crawler is stacked full of panels and supplies for the other camps. The one with me, Madge and Denim is in the back. It's about half full of things, leaving plenty of room for us. Holly and Janis are in the crawler in front of us and in front of them are Zar and Jo. It's slow going on the dirt road but when we get down to the main road it's smooth sailing.

We cruise along at a pretty good clip, looking around and talking, when all of a sudden Zar throws up his hand signaling us to stop and Cinn gives a warning in a low growl. I put on the brakes from our car so the train doesn't crash. Brakes are a new development on these crawlers. We used to just cut the power and let them stop on their own. They're like bike brakes and they work pretty well.

When the train stops we get out our dart guns. We all have one except Denim. I walk down to talk to Zar and see what's going on. There's a big tree trunk lying across the road. There had been no rain or big wind of late so we have to figure it's an ambush. Sure enough six guys come out of the woods with bandanas half covering their faces. I recognize one of them right away as one of the stooges from The Farm. I jog back to our crawler and tell Madge and Denim to stay down while we go over to talk to them. I try to stay calm. Denim's scared enough and Madge keeps looking around like she expects more of them to come out on both sides of the road. But there aren't more of them, thank God. There are only these six guys standing in front of us.

Zar and I walk toward them stopping about twenty paces short. I tell one of them I know exactly who he is. I inform them all there's no way in the world we will be giving up our cargo. We aren't giving up anything and if they know what's best they'll clear that log off the road and go back the way they came.

The next thing you know Cinn takes off running as one of the men throws a hatchet in my direction. I duck it and Zar plugs the man with a dart to the chest. We watch his knees wobble like he's made of jello and then he falls to his face and the rest of them take off running. It's something to see a large man crumble like that and I'm hoping he isn't dead. What he was doing is wrong but he doesn't deserve to die over it.

Zar looks him over and checks his pulse as he lies sprawled out on the ground. He's still breathing so we tie him up by his wrists and ankles and put him on a crawler. We pull off his bandana and see that it's the same bald headed man that did a lot of yelling back at The Farm. I figure Connelly must have sent him so we decide to take him back there to find out what's going on and deal with it.

It takes nearly half a day to roll that log off the road. Some other folks come by in their own crawler and help out. By the time we've finished it's already near sundown so we make camp a little ways down, the first place we can turn off that's safe or so we think.

We see two men hanging from a tree with a sign on them that reads: Thieves. Madge covers Denim's eyes but he sees it clear as day. Jo says it's a sign and a warning. Things may be changing for the better but it's still dangerous and we'd better take care.

I recognize those men. I know them – one from The Farm and the other from the Bridge Camp. They're good workers and I'm pretty certain they aren't thieves. What they were doing on this road I don't know. Maybe something terrible had happened. Maybe circumstances made them desperate. One thing I've learned is that there comes a time when any man will steal. You do what you have to do to keep your family or yourself from starving.

We're really disappointed. We've all traveled this road. We send patrols down this road. If it still isn't safe, what road is? Maybe we haven't made nearly as much progress as we think. Maybe we never will.

We cut them down and bury them in shallow graves with a pile of stones for markers. Zar says a prayer and talks about how hard it is just to live and it's understandable if some people turn to robbing and stealing things. It's wrong of course but it's still understandable.

The man we had tied up wakes up after a while and admits that the Boss Man sent him and his crew of misfits to ambush us. He says Connelly knew which way we'd be coming. They had a look out up in a tree so they knew when to let that log fall on the road. He says they weren't planning on hurting anyone. Connelly just wants to put a scare in us and take our stuff. He tells us they were planning to take it in the back way so the workers wouldn't see what was going on.

I don't believe the part about not hurting anyone and remind him about that hatchet. The man just shrugs his shoulders and says: *There's no accounting for the actions of low-life thieves.* Holly says he's damn lucky to be alive and tells him about the men who were hanged as thieves. The man doesn't know what to say about that. He knows.

Everyone takes turns standing watch during the night just in case one of his partners is still around looking for trouble. Nothing happens. It seems they've learned their lesson. I have to admit Carlin's dart guns work well – almost too well.

We encounter no more problems the rest of the way. We camp out with people we know. We had set up campgrounds up and down this road. We had two other kids about Denim's age at one camp. They hang out and talk. Denim tells them about the thieves being hanged and the ambush and their eyes get wide and Denim thinks they don't believe him so he tells them we have one of the ambushers tied up. So they all go over to look at him. The man goes quiet like he's sad and sorry at the same time. There was some talk about letting him go but I argue it's important we take him back to The Farm. One of the kids asks him if he's a thief. He just shrugs and says he'll tell them all about it if they untie him. Holly comes over and tells them to leave the man alone. The last thing we need is to worry over some kids who don't know what's going on. He tells them the man just might kill a few kids if he has to in order to escape. He doesn't have to say it again.

When we finally get back to The Farm we find out the word travels faster than we do. The workers are waiting for us and they know all about the man we have tied up as a prisoner. They haul him off and interrogate him. There's some loud talking and yelling before we haul him up to the big house where Boss Man Connelly looks like he ate something bad as soon as he sees the man's face.

Connelly is clearly flustered. He keeps looking at his wife and kids and the thugs who are supposed to protect him but they aren't moving a muscle. He goes from saying it's all a misunderstanding to saying it's a mistake to agreeing with almost everything Leon says. The truth is a hard thing to deny when it stares you right in the eyes. Even Connelly knows there's nothing he can say. There are no more lies that can help his cause. It's time to settle the account.

I ask Leon to put things on hold until after I get back from the neighborhood. I feel it's up to us to establish some working system of justice. I want to give it some thought, take care of business at home, and then come back to set up the trial. I ask him to keep the witness locked up until then. Leon thinks it over and talks to the others before he agrees.

We stay for a couple days to get things going with the solar panels and to make sure there's no more trouble. I tell Leon if anything goes wrong they should send a runner and we'll get help there straight away.

From there we move on to the Bridge Camp where Sugar is waiting, eager to greet us. He's heard about all the things we've been through and he tell us he's sorry.

He says we all have a part to play in making the roads safer and promises they'll do their part. Like The Farm they've been waiting for supplies and he's more than pleased to get them. He tells us everything's fine back home though some people are losing their patience with Carlin. We stay the night and eat a good meal in a brand new house constructed with their own special bricks. It's masterful work. It's amazing what good people can accomplish if you just stay out of the way.

We make our way home in the morning. I don't think anyone is happier than Denim. It was a great adventure but he's tired to his toes and ready to rest. The family is happy to see us all but especially him. We almost forgot that he ran off without permission.

They had every right to be angry but they weren't. They have a cake and everyone is in a celebratory mood. Grandma Grace gives him a big hug and asks him if he missed her like she missed him. He almost cries. The last time he saw his grandmother he wasn't even sure she knew who he was. Grace asks him if he's sorry he ran off and he says yes even though it isn't exactly true.

The truth is: He had the best time of his life. No matter what happens down the line he wouldn't trade it for anything. Madge sits him down and tells him:

*These are your memories. They're your most valuable possessions and you should hang on to them as long as you can.*

He promises he will. The truth is he doesn't see how he has any other choice.

# THE TRIAL

Leon says he knew that the Boss Man was up to something and there's no way he's going to get away with it. He tells me they've talked to the authorities already and no one cares who runs the place as long as it gets done. They're down to their last spot of patience and the next time he tries something like this he and his family will be out on the street and it'd fall on his shoulders.

After we brought Connelly's thug back and told them what had happened, they made a plan to inspect Connelly's private warehouse to see what he'd stolen from people. Sure enough they found a lot of things, including solar panels and roofing supplies.

*He's no better than any common thief.*

All along they had had to deal with the Boss Man and he fought them every way he could without a direct confrontation. By that time he knew full well he'd lose if he picked a fight straight up so he found other ways to try to gain back the power he'd lost. It didn't matter that he and his family had plenty and didn't have to work. It comes down to power every time. He told the workers it was still his property and they had no authority to put up buildings he didn't want built.

Leon told him his property rights had been suspended for the public good. If he didn't like it he could take it to court. They had someone on his trail everywhere he went. He had his route of trading partners and they wrote it all down. When the Boss Man went to the authorities, they went to the authorities.

The fact is the authorities have no problem with anything that goes on at The Farm as long as the food is delivered where it's contracted in a timely manner. When Connelly tried to stop deliveries the workers took over the operation. There were a number of times when the local volunteer police force showed up to check out what the Boss Man had told them. The workers showed them what they were doing and what they were building and the police told Connelly he was nuts if he thought they were going to stop them.

*It's a clean operation. Solid as a rock. Efficient. You're getting your profits and everyone else is getting what they paid for. So where's the problem?*

They tell him to step back, take it easy and enjoy life while he can. Times are hard for most people but not for him. He has no grounds for complaint.

If you think that would be the end of it you'd be wrong. They had any number of incidents that under any other circumstances would have called for swift and decisive action but the workers played it cautious. Connelly's goons harassed them and they went about their business. He sabotaged their work and they made repairs. At one point they thought he put something in the drinking water to make them sick so they boiled the water and kept a better watch.

Some of the workers went off and never made it

back to camp, never said a word to anyone. Leon and his fellow workers had their suspicions but they kept on working. They were afraid that if they took him out or burned down his house like some of them wanted to do the authorities would have no choice but to come down hard on them. They had heard stories about the military coming into situations and wiping people out. They figured it was only rumors at the time but they weren't about taking chances. There would come a time when they found out it was true.

Now it's all come to a head. We have one of Connelly's hired thugs, a nasty bald-headed piece of work by the name of Smitty, tied up and gagged. We tell the whole story from the ambush to the hangings. Leon says it reminds him of an old Billie Holliday song: *Strange fruit hanging from the Sycamore tree.* That song always brings out the anger in him. Some of the workers know one of the hanged men from the Bridge Camp and all of them know Paco. He was one of their own. *As hard a worker as ever toiled on God's green earth* is the way Leon tells it. It seems clear to everyone that Connelly had gone too far. If Leon had his way, he probably would have hanged Smitty from the nearest tree and then he'd have marched the whole lot of them over to that pretty white house, dragged that son of a bitch out and hanged him in front of his own family. Then he'd have burned the house to the ground. To hell with the consequences!

The alliance is facing a new challenge and now everyone knows who's behind it: Frank Connelly, owner-proprietor of The Farm. At some level I understand his frustration. This is his place and he's used to doing business a certain way. That he capitalized on hard times is a strike against him. The Farm is one of the few places that still have jobs. According to the laws of free enterprise he has every right to call the shots. If he wants to take advantage of the situation, if people are willing to work for food and a place to sleep, that's nobody's business. If people are willing to be slaves (for that's what they were) that's their own business.

The only problem is human nature and several thousand years of evolution. People have a natural aversion to slavery.

From his point of view Connelly is entitled to make a profit any way he can but like so many others of his bent he went too far. With his back against the wall, when he should have paused to take account, he went even further. He sent his thugs to ambush their solar train and that was only the beginning of his transgressions.

Smitty is a piece of work. He could have gone either way but he chose to link up with Connelly. He has no loyalty to his employer. He's a bad man with a nasty disposition. He doesn't like anyone and he'll take any man's reward to do his dirty work. Connelly paid in gas and food rations. That's good enough for Smitty.

The workers offer him mercy and he takes it without a pause. He sings like a nightingale. He confides that Connelly is behind it and his orders were to cause as much trouble as possible. They ask him if that includes killing people and Smitty nods. He says he hasn't killed anyone but he wouldn't be surprised if others have. He says they're a ragtag bunch of rats and thugs and some of them are probably in it just for the blood.

We uncovered the truth of his confessional when we

found those two men hanging from an oak tree. One of them was just a kid named Java from the Bridge Camp. He was joyful and full of energy, smart and eager to learn. He made friends everywhere he went and everywhere he went he was welcomed as a brother. Connelly wanted us all to believe he was a thief.

Well, he wasn't a thief and neither was his friend Paco from The Farm. He was an older man, quiet and a hard worker. His friends say he was fluent in Spanish but he struggled in English. He'd come north looking for work just before hard times hit. He was trying to make his way back to his family down south when he found The Farm and decided to stay and help out. He liked what they were building and he planned to bring his wife and children there as soon as it was safe. He would never make that trip now and no one but his dead friend Java knew where his family was.

Smitty swears he had nothing to do with it and we believe him. He's a nasty piece of work but he isn't a killer. We'd never know for sure but we're as sure as we can be that Connelly has blood on his hands. So we took Smitty back to The Farm as a witness with the intent to put Boss Man Connelly on trial.

Thank God we got here because there are a whole lot of angry people who feel the same as Leon does. They're filled with rage and itching for revenge. It's the way of their people. It's the way Leon was raised. *You take one of mine, we take three of yours. You take two and we take ten.* On and on. It never ends. It's the Hatfield's and McCoy's or Israel and the Palestinians all over again. It's one of the reasons this world got so fucked up. Tribalism, blood vengeance, no mercy.

It takes a while. Leon is stubborn about these

things. But in the end we convince him and most of the others. I tell them this is a test. It just might be the most important decision they will ever make: Whether they are going to be a community governed by laws or by men, by reason or by emotion. *I know both of the men we found hanging from an oak tree out there. It could have been me and Madge and Denim. But I don't believe in blood vengeance. I believe in justice. I believe in protecting the community but that's all.* I don't say so but I would have to turn my back on The Farm if they make what I consider the wrong choice. I want no part of mob rule or justice by revenge and neither does Zar or Holly or Madge or Jo or any of the others from the Sun Camp. It's the way of *our* people.

In the end they agree to do it our way. We will have a trial. We try to make it as formal as possible. We write it all down on paper so there's a record of what we do. I'm nominated to serve as judge but I have to refuse on the grounds of personal bias. The truth is we're all biased but some are more so than others. We do the best we can under the circumstances. Some of the workers don't want a judge or a jury at all. They want an immediate vote, the result of which is clear. It's the same as no trial at all. They want to string him up, an eye for an eye, in a spectacle of vengeance and they say so loud and strong. After a lot of discussion Jo is appointed judge, Leon represents the workers, Janis represents Connelly and Zar stands for Smitty. I volunteer as court recorder and take notes from beginning to end. We decide seven is as good a number as any and chose seven jurors. The majority decides the verdict.

The trial is in two phases: the first is without Connelly in the community center and the second is with the accused, confronting him face to face in his own house. We take witnesses and everyone gets their say. Half a dozen take the stand to say they've heard Connelly threaten to kill someone. Others testify they've seen Connelly and his thugs haul people to the shed out back, heard the screams of people being tortured, and on a couple of occasions watched them carry a body off to be buried out in the woods.

Janis argues that most of the testimony is based on hearsay and conjecture. No one had actually seen the bodies or knew where they were buried. She says that this trial is not about the past but about the two men that were hanged by the side of the road. She says that Smitty could not be trusted because he's just trying to save his own skin. Zar counters that Smitty has nothing to gain by implicating Connelly. It doesn't make him any more or less guilty of what he had done. Leon says we have to consider the character of the accused and a history of violent crimes is the best way to reveal his character.

In the end, after several hours of testimony and arguments for and against, the jury decides by unanimous vote that Connelly is guilty of sponsoring an ambush and causing two innocent men to be hanged. Smitty is found guilty of taking part in an ambush but he cannot be held accountable for the hangings.

Next we have to decide what to do about it. We talk for two more hours about what punishment we could rightly dish out. Leon argues hard and long that Boss Man Connelly ought to be hanged. He took two innocent lives and for all we know maybe more. If they let him live who's to say what he might or might not do? Give him a chance and he might take another life.

He might take out the whole community just to spite us. That's the way of *his* people.

We know we will have to hear from Connelly first but we also have to be prepared to act on the assumption that his testimony will not change our verdict. The penalty has to be carried out immediately or Connelly will hire his thugs and start a war.

It's a heated discussion. Almost all of us agree that the best way to deal with Smitty is to banish him. We will let him go but if anyone ever sees him again he will pay the price.

We're not in agreement on Connelly. Leon speaks out for hanging and I speak out just as strong against it. I was against the death penalty before hard times and I remain against it. The interest of the community is to insure that harm will not be inflicted on its people. If killing someone is the only way to prevent harm then it is justified but if it's not necessary then it's wrong. It's up to the people to decide whether or not it's necessary to protect the community. But if they can protect the community by other means then they should do so. I believe that they can protect the community without killing. I don't believe in an eye for an eye. I argue that when a society kills a killer it stoops down to the same level. If we take a life there will be a price to pay. Friends and family will bear a grudge that will be played out in years to come in ways we can't even imagine. It was the way of the world before hard times and it's time for a change.

My words seem to get to Leon. He thinks back to his old neighborhood in the city. He thinks about the gangs and the code of honor and all that bullshit that kept them fighting and hating each other long past the time anyone could remember what started it all. So he gives in and one by one he wins them all over. It's time for a new way and The Farm will be a part of it.

We talk it out and finally decide that the best way to protect the community is to confine Connelly to his home. The other members of the family will be able to come and go as they please as long as someone escorts them to make sure they aren't carrying orders or bribes from the boss. They will post guards around the clock to make sure no one enters and no one leaves without an escort. They will take his rations and therefore his means of hiring thugs as penalty for his crimes. It's a hard decision and a close vote but my side prevails.

We won't take his life but we will make damn sure he won't take another. He can live out his life in his pretty white house and his family can stay with him or not but he will never leave.

The entire community with Smitty still tied up and defiant as the day he was born confronts Connelly at the big house. We're armed and prepared to act. Connelly never denies hiring his thugs to carry out his dirty work. He only says that Smitty's a lying sack of shit and swears he'll have his revenge. When all is said, he only confirms that our decision is just. We inform him that he has been found guilty of sponsoring a crime and causing the death of two innocent men, that he will be confined permanently to his home and that his rations and possessions of value now belong to the community at large. His thugs stand down. They know their time at The Farm is coming to an end. One by one they peel off and go their own ways.

I tell Leon I'll take the case to the authorities and explain it to them so they can understand and that's just what I did. There's no more trouble over it. The truth is the authorities are probably just as happy as the workers that Boss Man Connelly is out of the picture. They can deal directly with Leon and the labor force without some greedy middleman angling for profits. Everyone wins.

Things go well after that. The Farm keeps growing. They hire more and more people willing to work for a living and deliver more and more food to people who are hungry. They put all their workers up in nice sturdy homes, welcome their families and see to it their needs are provided for. They have a working partnership with the Bridge Camp, the Sun Camp, the old neighborhood and a few other communities as time goes by and every one of them is better off for it. They offer a fair deal. They have rules and expectations but if you can't live with that you can leave any time you want.

They build a school and take care of the kids from early on. They have arts and theater and music. If you want to learn a trade they have skilled workers willing to teach you. After the trial, they have a court of law and a means of settling differences. If the workers or anyone else has a grievance they can take it to a vote. If people aren't happy with the leaders they have they have the right to call an election and choose new ones. They stand strong for majority rule.

The Farm belongs to the people who work the land and their former boss is now their captive. No one can say what would have happened if we hadn't come along to help. Maybe it was inevitable but even the inevitable can take a long time and a whole lot of suffering. Blacks in the south took hundreds of years to win their freedom and hundreds more to gain anything resembling equal rights. It took women even longer just to get the vote and the job of achieving equal treatment is nowhere near done. Maybe we just pushed history forward a little. Maybe that's the best any of us can do. And maybe that's enough.

# REBUILDING

The day Sugar showed up with his work crew Carlin put them to work. We had plans to rebuild the family home and set up a community center in the space left vacant by the families that stayed with the military. After that we would go about building a security wall and guard towers. That day seems a long way off.

The first thing we have to do is clear away the burnt out wreckage. The whole neighborhood pitches in but the hardest workers are the men and women of the Bridge crew. Being around them, talking to them and sweating with them on a daily basis changes what Carlin and his friends think about the people who ended up under that bridge and thousands just like them. Like a lot of people, Carlin figured they were all losers – drug addicts and bums. It goes to show over and over things aren't the way we think they are. Working with Sugar changes the way Carlin and his buddies go about their business, too. The late night partying is done.

Eventually, instead of going home to the bridge every night Carlin asks them to stay. They provide meals, set up tents and tell them how much everyone appreciates their help. Sugar tells them about the new community they're building in the old orchards across the river and when they're done here there would be plenty of opportunity to return the favor. Carlin nods and begins to appreciate what we have in mind. Every community has something unique to offer. Every camp has people with different sets of knowledge and skills and experiences that are useful.

The Bridge Camp has hard workers, people who know what they're about and are not afraid to sweat. They have people who can carry their own weight and then some. The Farm community is dedicated to producing food. They produce more than they can eat. In this world, that makes them both valuable and vulnerable. They have what everyone needs. The Sun Camp has advanced technology, especially solar and wind power. All the communities outside the city have room to grow, room for more gardens, greenhouses, canning and storage facilities.

Being in the city the neighborhood has more tools and supplies than the other communities – wires, nails, screws, gaskets and pipes. In this new world where very few industries are still making products, everything is in short supply. The hardware stores were cleaned out early on. What remains is stored in tool sheds and garages. Every house in the suburbs has a garage full of treasures.

The more they think about it, the more they like the idea. They still have some services in the city – sewage, water treatment and some recycling – but as time goes by they've deteriorated. There's only so much you can do without a budget and without paid workers. It's only a matter of time until it all breaks down. It would only make sense to get out of the city then and they would need somewhere to go.

Whenever Carlin talks to Joan about these things she tells him they should have stayed with the military. At least they knew there would be enough to eat and no one could threaten them. She has a point but she doesn't realize that they would have expected him to join up as a soldier. It's something he could not do. After what he had seen there's no way he could ever be a part of it. He can't really explain it in a way that Joan will understand but he's changed. The only thing she understands is that they're working like slaves and struggling day to day, when they could have been safe and taken care of back at the base.

She brings it up every chance she gets, every evening before they go to sleep and every morning before they get up, so he finally lays it out for her. He tells her what happened in every brutal detail: Teenage kids shot in the head point blank, shot in the back so they couldn't run away, people screaming in horror before they were put out of their misery, bodies piled up and carted away. He tells her they want him to do what they had done. They want him to be one of them. He tells her she can go back if she wants but they'd probably turn her away. It's soldiers they want, not women and children. Joan cries and Carlin cries with her. In the strange way that crises sometimes bring people together, they're closer now than they have been in a long, long time. Finally she understands. She will never bring it up again.

They work hard on the house from sunrise to sunset. They make good progress and they have enough workers that they decide to start work on the community center as well. They use the foundation of the neighbor's house that had burned down and expand it so it can accommodate a larger structure. They work in crews and each one has a specialty. When the foundation is finished the crew goes down to the Bridge Camp and starts work there. Carlin goes with them a couple of times a week and he's amazed at what they're doing and how fast the work is going. He imagined they would use wood to build cabins or shacks out of wood and tin. Instead, they make structures out of some kind of bricks for the walls and clay tiles for roofs. Aware of what happened with the firebomb attacks, they want to avoid using flammable materials wherever possible.

Sugar tells him they have stocked a lot of bricks from abandoned structures but when they didn't have enough to cover their needs, they went to work on making their own. They use clay or mud from the riverbank, mix it with sand, stone, plastic refuge, straw and the like until they came up with a mixture and a method that produces a strong brick that won't crumble in the heat or the rain. They seal it with a stucco mixture that has a grayish white look to it. They're pleasant to look at and far more stable, fireproof and resistant to weather than what Carlin had in mind for the neighborhood: traditional wood framed structures with dry wall or plywood with insulation.

Carlin asks if there's any chance they could supply the neighborhood with bricks and tiles. Sugar smiles and says they can, provided the neighborhood helps with the kiln problem. The one oven they have is ill suited to its purpose. Sugar is a sly and clever man in a good way. Carlin is sure he already knew they had a generator powered ceramic kiln in the neighborhood. It belongs to the Contreras family and Carlin's certain they're more than willing to fire it up for the cause. Carlin and Sugar seal the deal with a handshake and an unspoken agreement to work out the details as they go along.

From then on they use solar crawlers to transport bricks and tiles to the neighborhood for firing. They use what they need and transport the rest back to the Bridge Camp. Along the way they make friends and recruit workers. The Bridge Camp seems to be a magnet for bricklayers and masons and construction workers so they take them on. They become a part of a growing skilled labor force.

They have to draw a line somewhere and they leave that up to Sugar and his crew. There's only enough food for so many – even with their allotments. Carlin is there when Sugar has to tell a couple and their child they have to move on. The man is ready to fight but Sugar has such a soft touch and so much genuine affection he can only shake his head. Sugar sees to it they're fed and points them in the right direction the next day. He tells them about The Farm and says they might be able to take them in. They leave feeling Sugar has done all he can to help. They were treated with respect and that's more than they're used to these days. We learn later that The Farm found a place for them. They've become a part of the family and the alliance of communities thrives.

There are troublemakers too. Everywhere you go there's someone who wants something for nothing. There are bullies, punks and thugs who think they're entitled to take whatever you have just because they can. There's always someone who thinks he's big and bad enough to have his way even if it means running right over you.

On one occasion Sugar was running a load of bricks out to the Bridge Camp and a group of four or five scrawny looking men jump out from the bushes with clubs. The work crew holds up their baseball bats and pipes and the would-be hijackers fold right back in to where they came from. Another group has rocks and wants to stop a big crawler made for hauling. Anyone who had driven a crawler at that time knows the only way to stop one was to cover the ray collector and wait. Even then it took its own good time.

Sugar yells at them: *We ain't stopping but you're welcome to follow us where we're going!* They left them alone. The fact is: Nobody has much use for what they're hauling anyway.

The Bridge Camp got its crawler (they called it a solar hauler) from the Sun Camp. Sugar tells me they have another one coming. My plan is working. The communities are finding ways to work together that benefit everyone. The Bridge Camp has already sent a crew of brick makers and masons down to the Sun Camp to help them develop their own mixture using local resources.

It's midsummer and the weather is baking hot. Every summer seems hotter than the last. It's so hot you can't work without a constant supply of water. We carry leather pouches and take breaks every hour: forty-five minutes on and fifteen off. We have four walls up and a roof framed when a supply of solar and insulation panels arrives on a hauler. The panels hook together with an overlap that repels rain and seals the roof airtight. Sugar says it's the greatest invention he's seen in fifty years of engineering. It takes two working days to put the roof in place and when they're done it's as cool as an air conditioned home inside.

That's when everyone starts calling them the Sun Camp because of their mastery of solar technology. Every day there are more and more crawlers and they're getting better. Most of them (and all of the best) come from the Sun Camp.

People from the surrounding neighborhoods start coming to watch as we finish up the house and continue working on the community center. We assign a couple of people to answer their questions. The combination of the Bridge Camp's masonry and the Sun Camp's solar technology provides a perfect home for a new age, a completely self-sufficient structure with all the modern conveniences.

When the workday's done they discuss expanding the community by opening it up to surrounding neighborhoods. They talk about security interests and building a wall to protect the neighborhood from outsiders. It's a lot to consider but once they see what can be accomplished everyone is interested.

It seems that the neighborhood is getting more than their share of benefits from the alliance with other communities. That may be. But there is one other contribution they came up with that makes a difference. It's not something anyone likes to talk about but after the attack on the neighborhood they poured their knowledge and resources into weaponry. They have every description of bow and arrow, firebombs and spears.

One of the weapons they develop is an air compression gun that can stop a large man in his tracks. They can shoot darts or ball bearings. They can treat the load with chemical compounds that can burn with pain, paralyze or kill. When they realize that others will develop similar weapons they work on uniforms and vests that can repel them.

Of course the neighborhood still has guns, rifles and ammunition as well. You can be sure they aren't the only ones. It's a dirty little secret. But if the authorities catch wind of a shooting or an explosion of any kind, the military comes down on you full force. They won't take that chance unless it's absolutely necessary. No one wants to take that chance. The wrath of an angry God awaits anyone who defies the law of firearms. They're kept locked away and hidden from view. They won't use them unless their lives depend on it.

They share their weapons technology with their partners in the alliance. Everyone has had a taste of what thugs can do when they want what you have. Some people protest but they come around. It's a necessary evil. Even Madge and I and our friends at the Sun Camp understand. No one wants to kill anyone. Well, I guess some people do. I thank God we're the exception. That's why we need soldiers and cops. It's a tough job but someone has to do it.

We've had a few occasions to use our weapons. On one we had a crew taking a load of bricks to The Farm on a trade for dried foods. Dried foods are about as valuable a commodity as there is. Someone apparently knew about the shipment and a gang of thieves, about a dozen or more, confronted them on a country road. The gang attempted to surround them. Carlin showed his dart gun and warned the man who seemed to be their leader, a big man with a full gray beard, strong as a horse, that it was loaded and there was more where it came from. The others stopped but the big man kept coming. He shot him in the gut and watched him drop to his knees and crumble to the ground. Just like the time I plugged the Boss Man stooge from The Farm, the rest of them backed off, leaving their leader right there in the road, gasping for air like a wounded beast. He's lucky to be alive. No one who ever sees or even hears about the neighborhood dart guns in action will ever go up against them again.

The day we return from our trip south it's midday in late July and a little overcast. The walls are up on the community center and they're putting the finishing touches on the house. There's a crowd of a hundred or more people. It's like a festival. We drive up on our solar crawler like heroes returning from war.

We're given a tour of the house and shown our rooms on the second floor. It's really one room with two divisions: They have two bedrooms with a living space in the middle. Carlin and Joan have the same space. Mildred, Bud and Grace have smaller quarters on the ground floor. It will accommodate all of us and still leave plenty of room for the gardens outside.

Madge and I are like proud parents. We're happy and gratified. This is our work as much as anyone's. It's my vision and Madge has worked hard to make it come true. Everyone is relieved and pleased that we've finally come home. They're relying on us to help build the community. Others are good at getting things done but we have a knack for selling the idea. Everywhere we go we generate enthusiasm. We invite people in and make them feel like it's their dream too. It is their dream. It belongs to all of us even if they weren't a part of it from the beginning.

They become a part of it. My vision becomes our vision. All the surrounding neighborhoods want to join. What begins as one neighborhood becomes a village and the village becomes a town. We will prepare for all contingencies. With a little organization and lines of communication we will be able to respond to emergencies anywhere along the valley. We can defend ourselves from all intruders and at the same time provide for our needs.

The dream is becoming a reality.

## MOVING DAY

The longer we stay in the neighborhood the more I feel the pull of the Sun Camp. We've been away too long. We've done everything we can think of to get things moving in the right direction. Grace is settled in her new house. Uncle Bud and Aunt Mildred are as happy as they can be. Carlin and Joan are getting along better than they ever had even before hard times hit. The kids are going to the neighborhood school every day and doing well.

It's time for the family to go home. We know that the Sun Camp is where we want to live. Madge fell in love with the place on our visit and so did Denim. It's youthful and vibrant. It's on the cutting edge of a new earth-friendly technology. The people are thoughtful, accepting and idealistic. The ideas never stop flowing at the Sun Camp. The people are open to change and the community values are a mirror to our own. We've talked about the Sun Camp in such glowing terms that no one should be surprised by our decision to move there. Still, we have never made it official.

It's mid autumn when we sit down to dinner with a plan to make the announcement. Madge broaches the subject by talking about the weather and how good traveling days will soon come to an end. Carlin picks up the topic as if he knows what we intend. He says he expects we'll be moving on then and could someone please pass the salt. Everyone goes on eating and talking about nothing until a light goes off in Denim's mind:

*We're moving? To the Sun Camp? When?*

*Saturday morning if all goes well.*

We've arranged for three cruisers but we can't be certain they'll arrive on time. Grace is surprisingly composed. She says she saw it coming and prepared herself for the day. But then Charlie starts crying and Grace joins her, taking her into her arms to comfort her. Denim calls her a crybaby and tells her to get over it. We tell Denim to back down and spend the rest of the evening and most of the next day preparing Charlie for the move, explain that it isn't that far away and we can always visit, telling her how wonderful the Sun Camp is and how much fun she'll have making friends there. As children her age often do, she seems to understand and accept the idea and then the tears flow again. We finally tell her she can stay if she really wants to and that does the trick. As much as she loves her grandmother she wants to be with her parents.

We have a furnished cabin waiting for us so we pack only the things we don't want to be without. There really isn't much considering all that was lost in the fire. We have some books and works of art, some photographs and remembrances, a couple of baseball gloves, a bat and ball for Denim and his dad, and some handmade dolls for Charlie. The cruisers are already loaded with trade goods from the Bridge Camp when they arrive Saturday morning. We're a little surprised that so many of our neighbors are out on the street to see us off. Word travels quickly and every one of us has made good friends here. We say our goodbyes and promise we'll be back to visit sometime in the spring. After all, the Sun Camp is only two or three days down the road – less than that as conditions improve and the cruisers get faster – though in some ways it seems another world.

We have to stop by the Bridge Camp, of course, to say goodbye our friends there as well. I especially want to see Sugar. He's been making sounds about hitting the road again and he's getting on in years so I can't be sure we'll ever see him again. Sugar is a good friend, the best, and as good a man as I've ever met. I want to tell him what he already knows: that he's welcome at our home any time anywhere under any circumstance.

Sugar's already packed up and ready to move out. I offer him a ride knowing he won't take it. He's stubborn in that way. If he's on the road he's on the road and doesn't want any rides from friends. I'm pleased to see he's found a new companion: a big husky Sheppard mix that tows to his side. She will serve him well and protect him if he runs into trouble. Sugar has always loved dogs and they have a special bond. He tells us they're heading north for one last adventure before he calls it a journey.

We all give him a hug and our best wishes along with a dozen others who gather around. Then we start off south. In the new solar cruisers it's only half a day to The Farm where we have plans to spend the night. It's tough going for Charlie who has only been out of town once since hard times hit. She isn't used to sitting still so we plan to take it slow and easy.

We're pleased to see how well things are going at

The Farm. Since the trial there have been no more troubles. Leon is the man in charge and he rules with a firm but gentle hand. When there are conflicts he doesn't argue or make threats. He just takes the matter to a vote of the community council. The council grew out of the trial.

Holly and Janis meet up with us at The Farm. We'll ride together the rest of the way. We've been caught off guard before and we don't want to take any risks with the kids along on this trip. Denim is maturing fast. He acts like he's an old hand and coaches Charlie on what to do all along the way. Charlie has her feet planted by then and she takes her cues from Denim. Madge and I are proud of them. With what they've seen and lived through, you'd think they'd grow up with a lot of problems to work out. Maybe it's too early to tell but it seems they're doing just fine. Right as rain in the spring.

Leon looks up at the sky when we leave and tells us a storm is coming in. We don't give it too much attention at the time. We have good, strong tents and rain gear so it doesn't seem a problem. If the rain gets heavy or the wind blows hard we'll just pull off the road and camp until it passes. Leon doesn't seem alarmed either. They need the water. It's no more than an acknowledgement, not a warning. So we say our goodbyes like we have so many times before and start down a familiar road. We don't expect any problems. A couple of days and we'll arrive at the Sun Camp to start a new life.

We're half way to the next campsite when the storm hits and it hits hard. Thunder, lightning, sheets of rain and two or three strong winds. We know we can't travel through it so we pull to the side of the road and hunker down to wait it out. The wind is blowing so hard we can't pitch a tent so we hitch a tarp to the cruisers, pull out some blankets, some nuts and dried fruits, and wait.

Denim is holding up pretty well. He gets a wide-eyed look when he's scared but he'd rather eat worms than admit it. It's harder for Charlie. She can't stop shivering. Madge holds her wrapped in a warm blanket and whispers it'll be all right. Cinn cuddles up next to her to give her warmth and it seems to help. But the wind won't let up. It sounds like a hurricane, roaring through the trees and channeling down the road. Limbs crack and fall on all sides, one of them landing just south of where we're huddled. We decide we have to find a better place to pitch a tent and wait it out – all night if necessary.

I remember the first time Cinn and I went down this road. We had to wait out a storm for three days. I hope it won't be as bad this time. At least we have people expecting us and friends who know where we are. The one thing we know beyond doubt is that no one will be traveling this road tonight. It will take a lot of work to clear it and repair the washouts. We hope for the best but we have to be prepared for the worst.

The first thing we need is a decent campsite. The road is like a canyon for the wind and if the trees are going to fall they'll fall in the road first. We know this road well. It's too far in either direction to make it to a prepared campsite but there is a spot maybe a mile down where a path leads to a small clearing. The new cruisers are designed to build to a certain speed and hold it and the brakes are designed to stop (as opposed to moderating speed) so we have to push and pull them with Holly and Janis out front clearing debris. We can't see but a few feet in front of us so it's slow going. After a short distance we regroup and decide to leave two of the cruisers behind. We repack and start off again when Cinn starts barking. There are two people huddled alongside the road with a scooter – a man and a woman caught in the same storm and relieved to see us. They have no idea where they are or where they're headed and they're not prepared for harsh weather. We invite them to join us and they gratefully accept.

We find the path and Holly and Janis scout out a decent campsite maybe two hundred yards off the road. It's shielded from the wind by an outcropping of rocks with room enough for two tents. We hide the cruiser and the scooter by the road and haul what we need down the trail. I carry Charlie who is just beginning to settle down. We pitch our tents, gather up some dry wood and kindling, dig out a circle, line it with stones and cover it so we can build a fire in the evening. Then we all gather under one tent.

Our visitors are a young couple that has spent the last few weeks traveling north from Pasadena. They introduce themselves as Vera and Tack. They've stuck to the side roads, picking up work for food and gas as they go along. There was a terrible earthquake in Los Angeles and the fires that followed sent a wave of refugees in all directions. It's the first we've heard about it. They're cold, hungry and almost out of gas. They have no tent, no rain gear and no place to go. It's a reminder that no matter how bad things seem there are always people who have it worse. A situation that for us is probably just an inconvenience, an adventure and a story we would tell down the line, might have been a disaster for our guests.

It's a wonder they've survived their journey. They

say there are camps everywhere and most of them are willing to help. Holly tells them our group belongs to such a community and they would be welcome to visit for as long as they need. At the least we can provide food and shelter until they get back on their feet. They give thanks and say they will do so if it isn't too much trouble. They both smile that knowing smile that says they trust the world to take care of them. We're happy to be a part of that world.

I often wonder if what we have accomplished at the Sun Camp, at the Bridge Camp, at The Farm and in the neighborhood, is happening other places. I wonder if after all we've been through we might not be better off with the world we create from the ruins. Do we really miss the 24-hour news cycle and the media obsession? Do we really miss the web? Do we really need massive international corporations to govern our lives, to program our values, to tell us where and how we should live? Do we really need a national government? Do we really need nations? From what we've heard what has happened here has also happened around the world so we don't have to worry about conquering armies. Eventually we would have to deal with that of course. Maybe that's how it all begins: Armies of defense breed armies of aggression and the cycle begins again. We must try to find another way.

The rain keeps pounding, tapping a steady drumbeat on the tent, and the wind keeps blowing but the lightning and thunder have eased off into the distance. Madge is worried that Charlie is a little warm but Janis says she's fine. She needs fluids and nourishment but she's otherwise fine. Janis has taken on the role of a healthcare provider at the Sun Camp and she's well respected. She's saved lives including mine. One of the things we've learned is that many of the drugs that were fed to people by pharmaceutical corporations are completely unnecessary and often harmful. At first there was general panic. People broke down doors and stole all the drugs they could. Then there were no more drugs. Some people suffered and some died but most of the people, the vast majority, discovered they were better off without their drug dependencies.

People with an instinct for healing like Janis have become experts in alternative health care, using herbs and diet to treat disease and illness. All of our communities have a healthcare center now that provides essential care for everyone. We are not prepared for surgery of course but that is not entirely bad either. Surgery is always dangerous and should only be done when there is no alternative. If surgery is necessary we'll do the best we can. There are no hospitals and no surgeons but there are books and there are capable people willing to learn.

Vera and Tack take turns telling us about their lives down south before and after the fall. That's what they call it: the fall. As if it was a descent from heaven to hell. They were college students, both studying art and music, and both heavily dependent on computer technology. They were media junkies who spent the first weeks and months after the fall in acute withdrawal. Vera says it was an addiction no different than an addiction to drugs. She knows because she had been addicted to painkillers as well.

The earthquake was catastrophic. It would have been catastrophic before the fall but after it was beyond anything they could imagine. There are no emergency services, no firefighters or functioning hospitals.

218

People are pretty much on their own. They heard rumors that it was measured at 7.9 on the Richter scale – a major quake. They had been sleeping in a squatters' apartment building when the rumbles began. They ran out into the street with thousands of others. When it all died down they went up to the roof and witnessed the destruction. There were fires from Hollywood and downtown LA to the San Fernando Valley. The major freeways were down or badly damaged. Masses of people were on the streets with no place to go. Vera and Tack took off while they still could.

It's true that even LA has communities that share their wealth and make the best of things, planting gardens, building greenhouses and shelters. But the gang problem down south is far worse than it is in the north. The authorities let them sort things out on their own for a long time and then they came down like a sledgehammer. The massacres started down south and worked their way north. People like Vera and Tack decided it was better to deal with the gangs on their own terms than to invite the authorities to intervene. The people of the north eventually came to the same conclusion.

When the rain eases we light a fire and make some tea. It's a dark night with just the sliver of a waning moon. We can hear the rushing waters of a nearby creek, swollen with rain, and the usual rustling of small animals and an occasional yap or howl that restores poor Charlie's state of fear and restarts the cycle of comforting. We settle in and enjoy an opportunity to tell someone new all about the communities we have helped to build. Vera and Tack seem to enjoy the telling though they have to wonder if the claims being made aren't a little exaggerated.

In the morning we have coffee before hiking back to the road to survey the damage. From our vantage point we can just glimpse how bad it really is. In addition to fallen trees and branches the roadside creek runs so high that portions of the road have collapsed. We know right away we won't be changing camps. We can be sure that our friends to the north and the south will send crews to clear the road but only after they take care of their own problems. We will do our part by clearing as much of the road as we can. That first day the best we can do is to clear enough of the road to retrieve the cruisers. We settle back in camp, gather some berries, eat some nuts and dried fruits, drink tea and talk about old times.

Late at night something strange happens. Holly is the first to notice it. Off in the distance to the west there's a light. We're all but certain it hadn't been there the night before. We've been traveling this road long enough to know that almost all of these country homes are abandoned. Those that still have someone living in them don't have electricity. If they run on a generator they wouldn't waste it by lighting up the whole house at night. They'd use candles or a lantern or some kind of solar light, anything that doesn't expend energy. This is different. It's maybe three miles out and it's lit up like Las Vegas without a care in the world.

We talk for quite a time about what or who it might be and what we should do about it. Holly wants to hike up there and take a closer look. Denim is all for it. After two days in camp with no other kids but his little sister to play with, he's about as bored as a boy can be. Everyone else thinks it would be wiser to wait until daylight. So that's what we do. It gives us something to think about through the night. We watch it hour after hour, a blast of white light in the desolate darkness. No rhyme or reason. Something else is strange about it. If someone is living or squatting there, the lights would go out at some point – at least in one room or another. But there is no change that we can see. None. The lights are on and they stay on. It's baffling.

Then Madge says something that kicks me in the gut: *What if the lights came on?*

I know what she means. Back in the early days when the grid first broke down and the lights went out along with all the appliances, the TVs, the refrigerators, the ovens and toasters, people went to bed every night praying that the lights would come back on in the morning. They never did. That's what Madge means: What if the lights came back on? What if the grid is back in operation? What if the media is back? What if the world as we once knew it has been reborn?

I can't explain how hard that thought hit me. I try but I can't. I'm nervous and scared. Now it's me who wants to hike up there in the middle of the night with the rain coming down and who knows what waiting for us. But Madge is able to talk some sense into me. If I go up there, Denim is going with me. I can take chances by myself – even if there's no point to it – but I can't take chances with Denim and Charlie.

So we sit here and wait, watching and imagining what we're seeing. I think I see a shadow moving and maybe I do. Maybe it's a cat or a dog or a possum. Cinn goes off by herself a couple of times that night. She comes back to camp and gives me a look that I swear says something like: *You won't believe this!*

It's a long hard night. We all think about the implications. We think about property rights, courts of law, police forces and the National Guard. We think about armies and war. We think about working for corporations and drilling oil for industrial plants and fuel-burning cars. We think about all our friends at the Sun Camp, The Farm and the Bridge Camp who don't own the land they work and plant and build new lives on. What will happen to them? What will happen to us? What will happen to the world we're creating?

Madge, Holly and Janis are quiet in their sleeplessness. The thought that the world as they know it will once again turn over haunts them just as it haunts me. Tomorrow suddenly becomes the ultimate mystery. What kind of world awaits us? What kind of a God would wait until now, when hope is reborn and a world of promise has emerged from the dust, only to pull it all back? Is it all just a joke? Is this the punch line? I've had my doubts before but this is different. I can't wrap my mind around it. I want to be happy. I want to welcome the return of civilization, the return of strip malls and gas stations and convenience stores and 12-screen cinemas and... but I can't. Everything is turned on its head. For so long I wanted to wake up from the nightmare of the great collapse to find it was just a dream. Now I want the long-awaited rescue to be the dream.

Vera and Tack have a different take. Most people do. They belong in the world they left behind. They want to go back. They want their internet cafes, national and international news on the hour, every hour. They want Hollywood movies, the World Series and the NBA finals. They want it all back. They want the new world to recede like a bad dream. They can hardly wait to explore the house of lights and Denim is right with them. Charlie senses my misgivings and it holds her in check. She isn't sure what to feel. She senses that something important and maybe dangerous is waiting in that country house but Denim catches the excitement of an explorer. Something new and dramatic is something he wants to be involved in and he wants to get there now. We have to keep an eye on him so he doesn't sneak off in the night.

We're up at dawn and the anxiety of the night has diminished. We're by then all but convinced there's no other logical explanation. The storm has passed. It's a bright autumn day. Golden leaves, still dripping water, are falling from majestic oak, maple and dogwood trees. The earth is glistening with moisture from the storm. We drink our tea and coffee under a spell of silence that accentuates the morning song of birds awakening to the day's activities. There's a buzz in the air that we have not heard in a very long time. It's the sound of electrical currents, imperceptible when it's constant but distinct after a long absence.

Tack and Vera announce that they're hiking up there and everyone falls in line. It's not a long hike – maybe half an hour. We soon find a path that leads directly to the house. It once served as a conduit for vehicles from the main road. It's overgrown now and in need of repair but it won't take much. Whoever left this house must have thought to cover the path from the road. In all these many months no one has seen it.

When we reach the house the first thing we notice is that the lights are still on including the porch light. There's an old Ford pickup rusting away in the driveway, its tires long since flat. There's no apparent activity but as we draw closer we can make out voices. It doesn't sound quite real.

"It's the television," someone says.

We knock on the door and no one answers so we walk in, clearing the cobwebs as we go. It's pretty clear what happened here. Despite the dust and webs, the place is tidy. The shelves are stocked with books. There are photographs and pictures on the walls. The refrigerator is empty and the cupboards are almost bare. They had two small children. When the grid went down they packed up what they needed and went to a shelter or relatives in town to wait for the crisis to pass. They hadn't bothered to turn anything off. Whatever happened to them, wherever they are, they never made it back.

I wonder if they might not have been better off staying. They could have planted a garden. They could have fished the creek. They could have survived out here. Who knows? Maybe they were foreclosed. Maybe they were afraid to be isolated from others. Maybe they feared for their safety. Now that it's over maybe they will finally find their way back home. That was what everyone wanted for so long: to find our way back home.

We sit down and listen to the broadcast of a 24-hour news station. It's the only broadcast available. The reporters announce that the nation's long nightmare is finally coming to an end. The grid is up over most of the country. Electrical services are coming back on line. Some of the nation's satellites are operative and others are being repaired. The government of the United States is back in place. Order is being restored in the cities and help is on the way. It's the same story in Europe and Asia and throughout the world. It's the day of the Phoenix, the day the lights came back on and the day civilization as we know it was reborn.

# HARD TIMES

There's a lot of talk about what happened and why. We take it in and let it go. It no longer seems to matter. I'm filled with misgivings. The full weight of what has transpired finally settles in my mind.

We have only begun to realize our vision of rebuilding the world. We would hear similar stories all over the country and in other countries as well where communities had taken a similar path toward free energy, a new social order and self-sufficiency without poisoning the planet. There are stories of communities banding together, overcoming hardships and forging a new way.

There are dark stories too: Stories of anarchy, lawlessness, massacres and oppression, stories of starvation and wars over food and water. The good and the bad are in counterbalance but it's the good that I focus on. When the government comes back on line everyone instinctively senses that the experiment is over. We will of course continue our work as best we can but the promise of a new world and our hope that it would grow and that others would join in the vision is over.

It had been only three years though it seems like a decade. The authorities and the media are still trying to figure out what happened. Some insist it began as a cyber attack and catapulted in waves to a worldwide breakdown. Others say it was a convergence of random circumstance that exploited our vulnerabilities. No matter the theory, they all want to assure us it can never happen again. But we all know it can and will. They're rebuilding the system as if they hadn't learned a thing.

Tack and Vera are ecstatic and the kids take their cues from them. The rest of us are numb. After a while

Denim wonders why we aren't happy like the people on television say we should be. I tell him I'm worried about what will happen next. Madge says it will be fine but we're worried about the future. We don't know what to do or where to go. I'm afraid the authorities will shut down the Sun Camp and the Bridge Camp and turn The Farm back over to Connelly. Denim narrows his eyes as he stretches his mind to grasp what I'm saying: *They wouldn't do that. Would they?*

I just shrug and shake my head but I know: *That's exactly what they'll do.*

Several days later we arrive at the Sun Camp where the mood is somber. We have a meeting in the community center. Everyone agrees the end days are upon us. It's only a matter of time. Once the authorities are back in place they will close the camp down. The question remaining is: What will we do and how will they respond? We can fight it but that will only postpone the inevitable.

We decide to document everything we've done and when the evacuation order comes we'll transport all the equipment, the blueprints, notes and plans to the university. Maybe someday they'll sponsor a project. Maybe they'll rebuild in honor of what we tried to accomplish. In the meantime we'll go on living as we had hoped to live – in a spirit of harmony and cooperation. We had built something rare and special and though it's destined not to last we're proud of our work. We have a right to be proud.

The order comes at the beginning of spring and we begin the dismantling process. The story is much the same at the Bridge Camp where they tried to get the landowner to leave the community up for worker's quarters but the landowner is determined to level it. It seems they don't want any reminders of what people can build without any assistance from the banks or the government. Sugar came back in time to see them plow it under. He never said a word but it broke his spirit. A few weeks later he decided to head back to Indiana.

Connelly sells The Farm to a corporate farming operation at his first opportunity. A fire burns the big white house down to the ground. No one is hurt and no one is ever prosecuted but all the workers were cleared out. Leon and Marge move down south where he gets a job as a foreman in a processing plant. They have a little girl and they're doing fine. We make plans to see them around Christmas time. We would make it something of a tradition.

I get a job with the government rebuilding public buildings and housing. I get involved in local politics. I even think about running for city council until I tire of the process. Carlin gets a job out of town and they move on while we stay with Grace in the house we'd built from scratch. There are legal complications but we manage to work things out. Grace is losing her memory but she's still alert and kind as ever. The kids are back in school and doing well. The family stays in touch with Zar and Holly, Janis and Jo and all the people from the Sun Camp but everyone goes their separate ways. The university claims their solar technologies and awards it to some oil company in exchange for a large donation. Zar and Holly start a solar cruiser business but it's caught up in litigation over rights.

Within a few years things are pretty much back to normal. The grid is back in operation, the web is back online and government has been restored throughout the land. The skies are gray and the water is brown but no one complains much. As long as the computers and the web and the media are up and running the people are content. Most people seem to like it this way but some of us can't help but look back and wonder what might have been. I suppose that kind of opportunity only comes along once in a century or so.

Madge says it's best to look forward and I know she's right. It *is* better in some ways. We're more aware of our fellow human beings. Most of us have learned on some level that we're all in this together so we had better start looking out for each other.

Just the same, every once in a while, on a Sunday morning when everyone else is still sleeping, I go down to the bridge just to sit and think and remember. It all seems so remote now, like a movie or a dream. For a moment in time we had it in our hands to change the world from the ground up and then it was gone.

The years roll by and I sit on my porch in wonder. The sun is just now setting on the far horizon. Madge and I live in the country now. In a touch of irony we ended up buying the place where the lights went on. Grace, Uncle Bud and Aunt Mildred are long gone. The kids have grown into fine upstanding citizens, strong willed and good hearted. They have their own homes and families now. Denim has a daughter named Margaret Grace and Charlie has a son named Stone Jr. Life goes on.

I've been reading through my notes from the dark years and trying to decide if there's a story in there that hasn't been told, wondering if I'm the man to tell it. It's a scattered tale, a lot of stories really, and I don't know if I'm up to it. Madge tells me it's my story and I'd better get on with it. I'm not going to live forever. As usual I know she's right.

I pick up my pen and lay words to paper:

*Dear Denim and Charlie:*

*This is my story. I want it to be my legacy to you and your generation, your children and theirs, for generations to come. I want people to know that there is another way. A long time ago in a place not unlike our world there was a chance and a choice. I want people to know, sure as a setting sun, that there will come another time and that possibility will exist again. I want you to be prepared.*

*See the world as you want it to be and never give up trying...*

In a flash the lights go out and a profound silence comes over the countryside, a silence I have not heard in many, many years. I sit here absolutely still and I sense that every animal in the forest is doing the same. Madge comes out with a candle and a strange look in her eyes.

"It's happening again."

# ABOUT THE AUTHOR

Jack Random has lived at once an ordinary and extraordinary life. His roots firmly planted in the fertile central valley of California, he has marched the streets in protest, haunted jazz town bars, read poetry in cafes and town squares, strutted his hour upon the stage, crisscrossed the country by air, rail, highway and thumb, mourned at Wounded Knee, gazed into the eyes of the crow at Grand Canyon, and paid tribute at the grave of Geronimo. He has labored in the fields of plenty, toiled on the assembly line, pursued higher education and attempted to enlighten children in the public schools. He has been a pilgrim and a seeker of truth. He is married to the love of his life. All the while he has chronicled his thoughts and revelations in words: plays, poetry, novels, stories and essays. His first novel *Ghost Dance Insurrection* (Jazzman Series) was originally published by Dry Bones Press (2000).

# OTHER BOOKS FROM CROW DOG PRESS

*Wasichu: The Killing Spirit* – A Novel by Jack Random. A modern day telling of the life of Crazy Horse recalls the history of Native America and its most revered leader.

*Number Nine: The Adventures of Jake Jones and Ruby Daulton* – A Novel by Jack Random. A woman on the run picks up a hitchhiker and takes us on an adventure that winds its way to New Orleans in the summer of Katrina.

*A Patriot Dirge* – A Novel by Jack Random. Political genius Roman Mason takes on the political and economic forces that rule our lives (Jazzman Series).

*Jazzman Chronicles: Volumes I–X* – Essays by Jack Random. Political commentaries from 2000 to 2014.

*A Mother's Story* – Stories, Art and Reflections by Artis Brown Miller. A mother of eight children reflects on a life of hardship and love.

*Pawns to Players: The Stairway Scandal* – A Novel by Jack Random. An aristocrat and a billionaire play a chess match to determine the fate of the American government.

*The Grand Canyon Zen Golf Tour* – A Memoir by Jack Random. Two friends embark on a journey of golf, music, poetry and family in the summer of 1993.

## COMING SOON

*Pawns to Players: A Match for the White House* – A Novel by Jack Random.

*Crow Dog Press*

www.ingramcontent.com/pod-product-compliance
Lightning Source LLC
Chambersburg PA
CBHW051432170626
46809CB00006B/2424